Paul stood up slowly.

"I feel sorry for you, Lisa. You're going to mess up your whole life without ever realizing what you've done. Come on, I'll drive you home."

They rode home in complete silence. Paul swung the car into the driveway, then leaned across Lisa to open the door, wanting her to get out.

Lisa turned to thank him, but before she could get the words out, Paul spoke, "Good-bye, Lisa."

Paul's words echoed through her head. It sounded as if he never wanted to see her again . . .

Caprice Romances from Tempo Books

A CAPRICE ROMANCE

A NEW LOVE FOR LISA

HARRIETTE
S. ABELS

TEMPO BOOKS, NEW YORK

A NEW LOVE FOR LISA

A Tempo Book / published by arrangement with
the author

PRINTING HISTORY
Tempo Original / July 1983
Second printing / November 1983

ISBN: 0-441-57169-7

"Caprice" and the stylized Caprice logo are trademarks
belonging to The Berkley Publishing Group.

Tempo Books are published by The Berkley Publishing Group,
200 Madison Avenue, New York, New York 10016.
Tempo Books are registered in the United States Patent Office.
PRINTED IN THE UNITED STATES OF AMERICA

CHAPTER ONE

The heat and smog of August smothered Los Angeles like a giant blanket. For days the distant foothills had been obscured by the heavy hanging pall of gray air, waiting for an errant breeze to appear and blow it away.

Lisa Laine looked out at the murky sky, then turned to watch the huge white moving van back into the driveway alongside their sprawling California ranch-style house. Two men jumped down from the high front cab and opened the rear doors of the van, lowering the metal tailgate to the blacktop drive, leaping up nimbly into the tightly packed interior of the huge truck.

Lisa opened the screened front door of the house and bent over to prop it open with a piece of loose paving brick from the front path. She frowned up at the smoggy sky, comparing it with the clear ocean air in the beach town they had just left.

Sighing, she tucked a loose strand of soft brown hair behind her ear, her wide brown eyes watching with interest as the men began the long arduous job of emptying the van.

One of the men waved to Lisa. "Is Mrs. Hubbard here?" he called.

Lisa felt her jaw tighten. She couldn't get used to hearing her mother called by her new name. All the years Lisa had been growing up, her mother was known as Mrs. Laine. Now she had married Dave Hubbard and she would never be Mrs. Laine again.

She called into the empty house to tell her mother that the van had arrived. A few minutes later her mother came hurrying out, a big apron wrapped around her waist and rubber gloves on her hands. She pulled them off and handed them to Lisa.

"I've finished the kitchen, honey," she said. "All that's left to do is the back bathroom. I'd appreciate it if you'd do it for me while I show the men where I want the furniture."

"Sure." Lisa took the gloves and went into the house.

Dave Hubbard stepped out of the master bedroom as Lisa walked by. "Did I hear the truck?" he asked.

Lisa nodded and kept walking toward the bathroom. Although she had known Dave for almost a year now, she had never dreamed that her mother would seriously consider marrying another man. When her mother had told her that she'd accepted Dave's proposal, and they were moving from the small beach community where Lisa had grown up to the Los Angeles metropolitan area, Lisa was stunned. She hated the idea of living in the big sprawling city—miles from the Pacific Ocean and a world away from the small-town, uncomplicated life she was used to.

Even after Lisa had seen their new house in a small community near Pasadena, and she realized that they were not going to be right in the heart of the city after all, her anger still had not been appeased.

As Lisa sprinkled scouring powder in the big white tub and rubbed vigorously with the cloth, the same angry thoughts kept whirling through her head. Why, after all these years, had her mother suddenly felt the need to remarry? True, she had been a widow for fifteen years, ever since Lisa was only a few months old, but they had always managed very well without a husband and father around. Lisa was sorry her real father had been killed in the Vietnam War, but since she had never known him, it was somehow not as if she had really lost a father; she had simply never had one.

Lisa rinsed out the big tub and started on the sink. She'd always thought her mother was perfectly happy. She'd had a good job as a legal secretary to an excellent lawyer. Between her mother's salary and her father's government insurance, they never had any real money problems.

Over the years her mother had occasional dates with different men but Lisa had never dreamed she would get serious with anyone.

And then Dave Hubbard came into their lives. A television production company chose their beach town as the background for a new comedy series. The building that Lisa's mother worked in was used as one of the regular background locations. The series was a big hit and it became an everyday occurrence to see the TV actors and crew shooting on the local streets.

Somehow her mother had met Dave Hubbard, the set designer for the show. As shooting progressed, Dave began showing a deep and serious interest in Sandra Laine. Before Lisa had realized what was happening, her mother and Dave were deeply involved.

3

Lisa couldn't believe the change that came over her mother. It was as if years had rolled away, and Lisa was suddenly forced to realize that her mother was still a young woman, not yet forty years of age, and a beautiful woman as well—even more so now that she was in love.

"In love," Lisa muttered under her breath as she attacked the tile floor with suds and rag. It was weird to think of her mother that way. But anyone seeing Sandra and Dave Hubbard together couldn't miss it. Their eyes clung in a special way, and their hands unconsciously reached for each other whenever they were close.

"Like a couple of kids," Lisa muttered. "It's embarrassing."

She gave the bathroom floor one good last wipe and took the bucket out to the service porch to empty the dirty water. She could hear the movers rolling the big pieces of furniture in through the front door and she hurried back to her own room to make sure they put everything where she wanted it.

As soon as the bed was set up she went to ask her mother where she would find the linens.

"Don't worry about it," her mother said. "Mrs. Potter should be here in a few minutes and she'll take care of making up the beds."

Lisa nodded and wandered back to her room. Mrs. Potter. Well, at least one good thing had come out of this marriage. Mrs. Potter had been Dave's housekeeper when he lived in his apartment at the marina. She stayed on after Dave and Sandra were married and had been commuting to the little house at the beach where the three of them had been living for the past six weeks.

Now they were miles away on the other side of the city, and Mrs. Potter, a widow with no family of her own to worry about, had moved into a small apartment in Pasadena that Sandra Hubbard found for her. She had been delighted when they asked her to continue in her old job.

In the few weeks they had known each other, Lisa and Mrs. Potter—"Potsy," as Lisa affectionately called the tiny English woman—had established a firm and lasting friendship. Potsy seemed to be the only one who understood how Lisa felt about this marriage of her mother to a stranger. Even though Potsy adored Dave Hubbard, she was still able to understand Lisa's feelings.

"It will all come right, love," she had assured Lisa in her strong British accent. "You'll see. Dave is a wonderful man, and you'll come to understand."

Lisa had merely smiled at the older woman, not answering. She was having enough trouble accepting the fact that she had to live in the same house with him from now on. She was sure the day would never come when she'd love him, but she wasn't going to tell Potsy that and upset her unnecessarily.

Lisa removed the leather-framed picture of her father from the drawer of her nightstand and set it in its usual place. The picture had always been in her room. For years her mother had placed a copy of the same photograph on her dressing table—but that disappeared when Dave Hubbard came into their lives. The night Lisa realized the picture was gone, she accused her mother of forgetting all about her father. It was the first time Lisa could ever remember her mother screaming at her.

"He's dead, Lisa," she cried. "He's been gone for fifteen years." The tears rolled down her mother's face. "My God, I can't even remember what he really looked like. Don't you understand? He's been nothing but a photograph sitting on that table.''

Her mother's words were horrifying, and Lisa ran from the room sobbing hysterically.

The subject had never been mentioned again, but the scene lay like a festering sore in Lisa's subconscious.

As she finished hanging the last of her blouses in the closet, she heard Potsy's voice coming from the kitchen and ran in to greet her. Potsy gave her a quick hug and pushed her toward the back door.

''You'll just be underfoot, love,'' she said. ''Give me a chance to get my pots and skillets put away or none of us will have dinner tonight.''

''Don't worry about it, Potsy.'' Dave's voice came from the doorway. ''We're all going out for a hamburger later. I certainly don't expect you to put a meal on the table tonight.''

Lisa looked at him obliquely over her shoulder. ''Call me if you need me, Potsy. I'll be in the back.''

She went out through the rear screen door, letting it slam behind her, and decided to take a quick tour of the back of the property that sloped down toward a flower garden and a small gazebo surrounded by beds of blooming roses.

A large boxwood hedge separated the yard from the property next door on the right. The hedge must have been very old, as it was several feet thick and the inner branches grew in a tangled density. Lisa followed it along the property line, pushing past the walls of the house and out to the front yard, where the hedge extended to the sidewalk.

The moving men were still busy lifting, rolling, and shoving the heavy boxes and furniture into the house. Lisa dropped down on the lawn, tucking her legs under her.

Suddenly, something landed on the back of her neck and a warm, wet tongue began to lick frantically at her ear.

"Scruffy! Scruffy! Get back here!" The voice called from over the hedge.

Lisa grabbed the small white body and pushed it off her shoulder. She wasn't crazy about dogs to begin with and she certainly didn't want some strange dog licking her ear.

A girl about her own age hurried around the other side of the hedge. Her long blond hair had been yanked back into a messy looking ponytail. A boy's shirt hung over her dirty, worn-looking jeans, and the cuffs flapped untidily over her bare feet.

"I'm sorry," she gasped as she picked up the squirming Scruffy. "He just loves people. We can't convince him that everyone doesn't feel that way about him."

Lisa couldn't help laughing. She straightened her long slender legs and stood up.

The girl stared at her curiously. "Are you going to live here?"

"Yes." Lisa nodded. "I'm Lisa Laine."

"Hi." The girl stuck out her hand and grabbed Lisa's, shaking it vigorously. "I'm Holly Webster. I live there." She pointed to the house next door. "How old are you?"

For a moment Lisa was taken aback by the other girl's bluntness, but then she decided it was simple curiosity on Holly's part.

"Fifteen," she said. "Almost sixteen, in a couple of months."

"Me too." Holly sounded pleased. "I mean, I was sixteen last month, so we're practically the same age."

Lisa was surprised. She had thought Holly was younger. Somehow Lisa had expected that the girls in this area would be more sophisticated and worldly than the

7

friends she had left at the beach. But Holly, if anything, was less sophisticated, and for some reason Lisa suddenly felt better about this new environment she had been thrust into.

"Are you a sophomore?" Holly asked eagerly, and when Lisa said yes, she nodded vigorously. "So am I. That's great. Maybe we'll have some classes together." She paused. "You are going to the local high school, aren't you?"

"Of course," Lisa said. "Where else would I go?"

"I don't know." Holly shrugged. "A lot of kids in this town go to private schools. I thought maybe . . ."

Lisa shook her head. "Not me. I wouldn't want to do that."

"Me either," Holly said. "Our school is great. You'll love it."

Lisa laughed. "That's putting it a little strongly, isn't it? I've never loved school yet."

"Oh, I wasn't talking about the classes." Holly's round flushed face grew serious. "I meant the kids. You know, guys and stuff. Don't worry, I'll introduce you to all of my friends."

Lisa suddenly felt shy. "Thank you," she said quietly. "That would be nice."

Holly stared at her intently for a moment. "You're very pretty. Do you know that?"

Lisa felt herself blushing. Holly certainly was blunt. Lisa had never known anyone quite like her.

"Thank you," she murmured again.

"I mean it," Holly assured her. "I always mean what I say. And I think you should tell people things like that, don't you? I mean, if somebody's pretty, or a guy is good-looking, I think you should let them know."

"Do you tell them bad things?" Lisa wasn't quite sure where this outspoken girl was coming from.

Holly snickered. "Yes, I'm afraid I do. My mom keeps telling me I shouldn't—she says I have to learn to watch my tongue. But I keep telling her, 'This is me. Take me or leave me.' And she doesn't have much choice." She laughed again. "She's stuck with me."

An old red P1800 Volvo came roaring up the street and swung into the driveway next door.

"That's Paul," Holly said. She jumped up and peered over the hedge.

"Hey, Paul," she yelled. "Come and meet our new neighbor."

Lisa rose slowly to her feet and looked into Holly's yard.

A long, lanky body was unfolding itself from the low sportscar. Then Paul Webster stood up and looked across the hedge at the two girls.

His hair was as blond as Holly's and his eyes as large and blue. High cheekbones narrowed into a firm chin, and his lips parted in a big smile, showing strong, even white teeth.

Lisa felt as if someone had hit her over the head. She knew she was staring but she couldn't help it. Slowly her eyes moved upward until they met his and she watched, stunned, as the smile slowly faded from his face. Lisa caught her breath.

Dimly, in the background, she heard Holly introducing them. But neither she nor Paul said a word for endless moments. Then Paul made a small movement, as if to shake off a spell. His wide grin reappeared.

"Hello, Lisa," he said. "It's nice to meet you." Two red spots appeared on his cheeks and he hurriedly looked down at his dirty T-shirt and jeans.

"Uh, excuse me," he stammered. "I have to go get cleaned up. I'll see you soon." He turned and loped into the house.

"Wow!" Holly breathed. "You made some impression on my big brother."

Lisa turned slowly to stare at the other girl. "Your big brother?"

"Yes. Paul." Holly began to giggle. "Wow!" she said again. "I've never seen two people react like that to each other."

"How . . . how old is Paul?" Lisa stammered.

"Seventeen," Holly said. "Almost eighteen. He's a senior this year."

"Does he, I mean, is he, uh . . ." Lisa didn't know how to get the words out but Holly got the message right away.

"Nope." She shook her head. "No girlfriend. At least, not one he's ever told me about. In fact, he's kind of busy. He doesn't date much."

"Do you?" Lisa asked.

"My mom only let me start dating this summer. Well, I don't really date," Holly said, "but there's a crowd of us who hang out together. We do lots of stuff like parties and the beach. You know, that kind of thing."

"You go to the beach from here?" Lisa asked.

"Sure, we go down all the time. Why?"

"Well, it's so far away." Lisa thought of how long the drive had taken that morning from their old house.

"No it isn't," Holly said. "It only takes about a half an hour."

Lisa realized that from here they must go to a different area along the Pacific than the town she had come from. It was good to know. Even if she didn't live there anymore, at least she'd be able to see her beloved beach once in a while.

Holly squatted down on the lawn and pulled Scruffy into her lap.

"Tell me about yourself," she said. "What do you do?"

Lisa wasn't quite sure what she meant. "I go to school." She shrugged. "I guess that's about it. How about you?"

"The same," Holly said. "I babysit once in a while, but most of the people around here have maids, so it's not exactly a lucrative profession. My dad's a doctor. What does your father do?"

Lisa suddenly felt cold. "Dave's not my father," she said. "He's my mother's husband. My father is dead."

"Oh." Holly's voice grew quiet. "Don't . . . don't you like Dave?"

Lisa shrugged. "I don't even know him. They've only been married about six weeks."

"Do you have sisters or brothers?" Holly asked.

"No." Lisa shook her head. "My father was killed in Vietnam when I was six months old. My parents had only been married a few months when he went overseas."

"Gosh, that's too bad." Holly reached out and touched Lisa's arm gently. "It must be rough growing up without a father."

"I never thought so," Lisa said. She gave a little laugh. "I guess if you've never had one, you don't know the difference. I suppose if it had been my mother who'd died it would have made a big difference. But a father . . ." Again she lifted a shoulder. "We got along fine without one."

11

Holly thought for a moment. "Yeah, I understand what you're saying. But I'll tell you"—she looked at Lisa and grinned—"having a dad like mine is great."

"Do you see much of him?" Lisa asked.

"Sure." Holly looked confused. "I see him all the time, why?"

"Well, I always heard that doctors are so busy their families never get to see them."

"Not my dad," Holly said. "He's always made time for us. For Paul and me. And for my mom, too. You'll see, Lisa, now that you have a father, it'll make a big difference."

Lisa stood up. "I told you. I don't have a father. My mother has a husband, and that's all he's ever going to be."

Holly got slowly to her feet. "Is there something wrong with him?" she whispered.

"He's okay, I guess." Lisa didn't have anything against Dave personally—other than the fact that he existed, that is. "He's a set designer for TV," she volunteered.

"Wow!" Holly exclaimed. It seemed to be her favorite expression. "That's terrific. Do you get to go to the studios? Do you get to visit the sets?"

"I guess I could if I wanted to," Lisa said. "But I've never asked."

"Do you think he'd ever let me go?" Holly wanted to know. "I'm a real TV nut. I'd love to see all that. What shows does he work on?"

Lisa mentioned the comedy that had originally brought Dave into their lives, and she could tell Holly was impressed.

"Lisa?" She heard her mother calling from the house. "Lisa, where are you?"

"I'd better go," Lisa sighed. "There's a lot to do setting up the house. I'd better help Potsy and my mother."

"Potsy?" Holly raised an eyebrow. "Who's that?"

Lisa explained about the housekeeper. "We inherited her with Dave."

"Don't you like her either?" Holly wanted to know.

"Sure I like her."

Holly shrugged. "I just wondered. After the way you were talking about him, I thought . . ."

"I don't blame Potsy because she worked for Dave," Lisa said. "It was just her job. And besides, she's a good cook." They both laughed.

"If you get settled in by tomorrow," Holly said, "maybe we could do something."

"Sure," Lisa agreed. "I'd like that."

Holly whistled for Scruffy, who was busy digging frantically at something under the hedge, and waved as she walked back toward her own house.

Lisa ambled slowly across the lawn toward the front door. Well, at least she had made a friend. She liked the friendly and open honesty of the other girl.

And Paul. . . . That strange feeling she had experienced came over her again in a rush. Her throat felt tight with excitement. She was glad that of all the houses in this new town, her mother and Dave had chosen the one next door to the Websters.

CHAPTER TWO

By Saturday of that week they were well settled into the new house.

Lisa was pleased with her room. She and her mother had chosen a pretty green and yellow floral spread and drapes that blended well with the off-white walls.

Dave and her mother were still busy selecting things for the rest of the house. Lisa had to admit that Dave had excellent taste in furnishings, but that was part of his profession. As a set designer he was involved with that type of work all the time.

Several times they had asked Lisa's opinion of a piece they were considering buying, but Lisa knew they didn't really care what she thought. They were just trying to make it appear that they were a normal family circle. It was all sham and pretense and Lisa didn't want any part of it.

Sandra was Dave's wife. She was also Lisa's mother. But the two things were separate, distinct, and Lisa intended to keep it that way. If Dave spoke to her, she answered him politely, but she never volunteered any conversation on her own. The man was of no interest to her, and she did not intend to give him a place in her life.

Potsy had tried several times to talk to her about it.

"What is it, love?" she asked. "Did he say something to you that you didn't like?"

"Of course not," Lisa answered. "You know he's very polite."

"He's also warm and understanding," Potsy said. "When my husband passed away I don't think I could have made it without Mr. Hubbard to turn to. And he loves your mother very much, Lisa. You only have to look at the two of them together to see it."

"I know." Lisa suddenly turned on her. "But she didn't need him to love. She had me. We've always had each other. Why did she suddenly have to find somebody else?"

"Ahh, so that's it, young one." Potsy reached out and touched Lisa's cheek gently. "But the love she has for her man has nothing to do with the love she holds for you. You're her child. But that's not enough."

"Oh, really?" Lisa knew her voice sounded shrill. "It was enough for fifteen years. What suddenly changed it?"

"She met Dave Hubbard," Potsy said simply. "That's all it takes, you know. Just two people meeting."

For a moment Lisa thought of Paul Webster, of the feeling that rushed through her when their eyes had met over the hedge. But that had been three days ago, and she hadn't seen anything of Paul since. She thought the feeling was mutual . . . obviously it hadn't been.

There was a knock on the back door and Lisa turned gratefully to it, glad to put a stop to the conversation with Potsy. When she opened the door Holly stood there,

Scruffy panting happily at her feet.

Holly had been over every day since the move and Lisa already felt as if she'd known her for years.

"How about it," Holly said now. "Are we going?"

"Going where?"

"Honestly, Lisa, I'm beginning to realize how absentminded you are." Holly sounded exasperated. "We said we'd go shopping up on Lake Street today. You were going to help me buy some makeup."

Lisa had discovered several years earlier that she had a knack for makeup. At her old school she worked on several school plays and became interested enough to go to the library and find some books on the subject.

When the television crew had arrived at their town, she quickly attached herself to the makeup and costume truck. The people who worked on it were very generous about showing her their techniques when they realized she was truly interested.

Although Lisa wore very little makeup herself, she practiced endless hours on her friends and on her mother. She learned how, with subtle color, to enhance her own natural good looks and she had promised Holly to show her how to do her face.

"I'll be ready in a minute," Lisa said, and ran to her room to run a comb through her hair and grab her purse.

They caught the bus several blocks away that would take them into Pasadena.

"Paul offered to drive us," Holly said as they settled into their seats, "but I figured we didn't want him hanging around all morning. He'd just be in the way."

Lisa was afraid to turn and look at her. For three days she had been dying to ask where he had been, but she was afraid to let on that she was interested. What if Holly said

17

something to Paul and he got annoyed? She'd be embarrassed to death. She'd never be able to face him again.

"You don't mind, do you?" Holly leaned over and peered into her face. "About taking the bus instead of getting a ride, I mean."

"No, no." Lisa hastened to assure her. "This is fine with me."

Holly's lips tucked into a little grin, but she didn't say anything. The bus let them out on a corner across from the department store where they were going to buy the cosmetics. After wandering past some of the store windows, Lisa led the way across the street.

"This is going to take a while," she said to Holly. "Let's get started."

It took about a half an hour for Lisa to select all of the things she wanted for Holly's transformation. She chose the colors carefully, trying a number of them out on Holly's hand until she found exactly the right shades.

"Okay," she finally breathed. "That's it, I think. Now let's go home and see what we can do with all of this."

"Sure," Holly agreed. "But first, let's go down to the Hamburger Shack and get something to eat."

"We can do that at home," Lisa said. "Potsy will make us a sandwich."

"That's silly," Holly said. "We're already here. It will only take a little while. Come on," she urged.

Lisa didn't understand why Holly was being so insistent, but she gave in and they walked down the tree-lined block to the restaurant.

As they walked through the door, Lisa spotted Paul sitting at a back table. As soon as he saw them he jumped up and waved, motioning them to come over.

"I thought you were never going to get here," he said.

18

He turned to Lisa. "Hi." His voice was soft. "Remember me?"

Lisa slid into her chair, her eyes never leaving his face. "Hello, Paul." She couldn't think of anything else to say.

"Surprise, surprise," Holly murmured under her breath, and Lisa shot her a look, suddenly realizing that this had all been arranged in advance.

She could feel her heart begin to pound. Did this mean that Paul had wanted to see her again, too? But he could have done that at home. Why hadn't he just come around the hedge and knocked on the door? She must be wrong. Maybe it was simply a scheme of Holly's to get them together again. In that case, Paul was probably as embarrassed as she was.

She looked at him from under her lashes. He didn't seem to be embarrassed. In fact, he and Holly were looking at a menu together and laughing over some silly remark Holly had made.

Lisa took a deep breath and picked up her own menu. The printing looked blurred and she gave her head a small shake, trying to clear her mind.

"The dragonburger is good," Paul said. "That is, if you like things that are hot, Lisa."

Lisa pasted a bright smile onto her face. "What's in it?" she asked.

"Chili. Do you like it?"

"Sure. I'm game."

Paul called over the young girl who was their waitress and ordered three dragonburgers, a double for himself. Holly and Paul ordered Cokes to go with it, but Lisa asked for iced tea.

"You should do the same," she said to Holly. "Cokes don't do much for the complexion."

19

"Hey, what's wrong with my complexion?" Holly ran her fingers over her smooth fair skin.

"Nothing right now," Lisa said, "but it'll catch up with you if you aren't careful. Listen, if I'm going to go to all the trouble of making you gorgeous, I expect you to cooperate."

Paul looked from one to the other. "What's going on here?"

Lisa started to tell him, but Holly quickly interrupted her. "He'll be the acid test, Lisa," she said. "If he notices anything, that means it'll be a big success."

Lisa's laugh was hesitant. She wasn't quite sure what Holly meant.

"I'm his sister, silly." Holly giggled. "He never really looks at me. Now if it were you . . ."

Lisa felt her cheeks redden and looked up gratefully as the waitress brought their hamburgers and drinks to the table.

After they had finished eating, Paul ushered them outside to the P1800 parked at the curb.

"Do you two have anything special planned for this afternoon?" he asked.

"What did you have in mind?" Holly encouraged.

He gestured over his shoulder. "There's a good science fiction flick playing up at the Capitol Theater. I thought maybe I'd treat you two if you want to go."

Holly looked at Lisa, one eyebrow raised. "Shall we postpone the beauty session?"

"It's up to you," Lisa said quietly. "Although there'll be plenty of time to do it after we get home." Fervently she hoped that Holly would agree. It meant they'd be able to spend the whole afternoon with Paul.

"Let's go then." A big smile lit Paul's face. "We'll leave the car here."

They walked the few blocks to the theater in the heat of the afternoon sun. The lobby felt cold when they walked in and Lisa shivered, rubbing her arms from the shock of the sudden change in temperature.

The lobby was filled with a noisy, chattering crowd. Many of them seemed to be friends of Paul and Holly, and Lisa was introduced to so many new faces that she couldn't keep the names straight.

"Do you like to sit close or far back?" Paul asked.

"It doesn't make any difference to me," Lisa said.

"He likes the back row," Holly declared. "I like to sit up front."

"Not too close," Lisa protested. "It hurts my neck if I have to look up."

Paul grabbed her hand. "You come with me." His touch was firm. "We're sitting in the back. Let Holly go wherever she likes."

"That's fine with me." Holly grinned at them. "See you later." She walked off, slinging her arm through another girl's and sauntering down the aisle.

"But, Paul," Lisa started to protest.

"What's the problem?"

"I . . . I really should go with Holly," Lisa stammered. "What will she think?"

"She'll think you don't like to sit down front because it hurts your neck," he said reasonably.

They found two seats in the center of the last row. As Lisa made herself comfortable, Paul said, "Save my place. I want to get some popcorn."

The lights in the theater were still up and Lisa looked

around. The theater was only half-full. Most of the patrons were teenagers or young children with their mothers. When Paul came back carrying two tubs of popcorn, he placed one in Lisa's lap, clutching the other to his chest. He quickly dug into the fluffly white kernels.

"It's good," he said. "Try it."

Lisa felt the rumblings of the dragonburger she had just finished and thought the last thing she needed was a tub of popcorn. But she slipped a few kernels into her mouth, chewing vigorously. It was good, hot and salty.

"Why aren't you working today?" she asked.

"I never do on weekends," Paul mumbled through a mouthful of popcorn. "I work on a construction crew for my uncle's company. We don't work on the weekends because it costs the customer double time."

"What do you do? Are you a carpenter, or . . ."

"Not exactly," Paul said. "Actually, I'm more of a gofer."

"A gopher?" Lisa asked.

"You know," Paul said, "go for . . . go for this, go for that."

Lisa had never heard the expression before and thought it hysterically funny.

"How long have you been doing it?" she asked when she finally stopped laughing.

"This is the first year," Paul answered. "I was never old enough before. But I'm interested in that kind of work."

"Building things, you mean?"

"Yeah." Paul nodded. "I work on all the sets for the plays we do at the high school."

"Oh." Lisa wondered if she should tell him about Dave. It felt strange to be bragging about her mother's new husband, but she was sure Paul would be interested.

"Did you know Dave is a set designer?" she asked.

Paul put his nearly empty popcorn container on the floor. "Who's Dave?"

"My . . . my mother's husband."

Paul pulled a handkerchief from his back pocket and wiped his hands. "You mean your stepfather."

Lisa slid down in her chair and propped her knees on the seat in front of her. "He isn't my stepfather," she said. "I told you. He's my mother's husband."

Paul looked down at her, a strange expression on his face. "Holly said you weren't too happy with the arrangement at home."

Lisa shrugged. "I'm not unhappy. I know I have to live with it."

"What's the matter with him?" Paul asked. "Is he mean?"

"Mean?" Lisa looked up at him. "Mean like in nasty?"

"Yeah." Paul nodded. "Doesn't he like you living with him and your mom?"

Lisa straightened up hurriedly. "Oh, it's nothing like that." She didn't want to leave a wrong impression in Paul's mind. "It's just that, well, my mother and I have been alone all these years. We got along fine. I guess I don't really understand why she got married."

Paul started to say something, but the house lights went down at that moment and the coming attractions flashed onto the screen. For the next two hours they sat enjoying the picture, an exciting science fiction epic with complex and spellbinding special effects. At one particularly tense point, Lisa let out a gasp and Paul reached over to grasp her hand reassuringly. He kept a firm grip on her fingers for the rest of the afternoon, not letting go until the film had ended and it was time to leave.

Holly rushed up the aisle to meet them and they walked out into the late afternoon sunlight. Paul's arm draped casually across Lisa's shoulder. Holly made no comment, but Lisa knew she had noticed it.

When they arrived back home, Lisa turned to Holly in the driveway.

"Would you like to come over to my room and we'll do the makeup?"

"Sure," Holly agreed. "I can't wait to be beautiful." They all laughed and Lisa looked at Paul.

"Thank you," she said quietly, "for the movie and . . . and everything."

He smiled gently. "Thank you for sitting with me." He paused. "And everything."

Flustered, Lisa turned away.

"Tell Mom I'll be next door," Holly called back to him as they walked around the hedge.

They were on their way down the driveway, heading for the back door, when a furry white object came hurtling behind them, yapping sharply. Holly leaned down and picked up the panting Scruffy, hugging him and letting him lick her neck and ear.

"You really love him, don't you?" Lisa asked, laughing.

"Sure I do. That's my pal," Holly said, setting him back down on the ground. "Don't you like dogs?"

"I've never had one. But I must admit, I'm getting kind of fond of this one."

Mrs. Potter was in the kitchen fixing dinner as they walked through. "Hi, Potsy," Lisa greeted her.

"Hello, love. Where have you been all day?"

Lisa told her and showed her the bag of cosmetics they were holding.

"We're going to do a remodeling job now." She looked around. "Where's Mom and . . . Dave?"

"Out shopping," Potsy said. "They should be home any minute."

Lisa ushered Holly into her room and sat her on a chair near the window. In a few minutes she was intent on the job in front of her.

"Hi." Lisa's mother smiled at them as she stuck her head in the room. "What's going on?"

"The transformation of Holly." Lisa laughed.

Dave's head peered over her mother's shoulder. "Is that light good enough, Lisa?" he asked.

"It's the best I can do," Lisa said coldly. "The lighting in this room isn't very good."

He came halfway into the room. "Why didn't you say something before?"

"It isn't important." She went on with what she was doing.

"Maybe I could fix something up for you." He looked over at the mirror above her dresser.

"Don't bother. I said it isn't important."

"Lisa."

She heard the note of pleading in her mother's voice but ignored it.

Her mother sighed and walked out of the room.

"Well," Dave said hesitantly, "I'll try to think of something." He went out, shutting the door behind him.

Holly looked at her strangely. "Why do you act like that with him? He seems to like you."

"I'm sure he does." Lisa's voice was noncommittal. "But I don't happen to care for him. Look"—she leaned back in her chair, giving an exasperated sigh—"he's got nothing to do with me, Holly. It doesn't make any difference whether I like him or not. My mother married him, I didn't."

"I don't think that's exactly true." Holly leaned forward and touched her arm. "You can't ever be a family, Lisa, if you keep acting like this."

"What makes you think we want to be a family? My mother and I were a family, and then he came along, and . . ."

Holly settled back in her chair. "Hey, I don't want to get into this. It's none of my business. Come on, finish me up so I can see how gorgeous I am."

When Lisa was through she led Holly over to the mirror on the opposite wall. The makeup she had applied was subtle but deft. Holly's blue eyes looked bigger and brighter. The foundation and blusher Lisa had applied brought out the silken tones of Holly's skin and shaped her round cheeks. She had also loosened Holly's hair from its normal tight ponytail, arranging it softly around her face.

"Some of that hair has to go, Holly," she said. "Will you trust me to trim it for you? Or else make an appointment with a good hairdresser and have it shaped."

"I can't believe what you've done to me," Holly breathed. "I don't look like me anymore."

"Don't you like it?" Lisa asked anxiously.

"Like it? I love it!" Holly shrieked. She turned and threw her arms around Lisa. "Thank you, thank you! It's terrific. Will you show me how you did it so I can do it myself?"

"Of course, that's the whole idea." Lisa grinned at her.

"You know the big difference?" Holly examined herself critically in the mirror. "I don't look twelve years old anymore. I mean, I'm sixteen—and now I look it!''

"Of course, this sort of makeup is only for dating."
Lisa cautioned. "I'll work out something simpler for you
for school. You don't want to walk around all day with
this stuff on your face."

"Right." Holly agreed. "Besides, my mom would kill
me."

"Lisa." Her mother's voice came through the closed
door. "Paul is here looking for Holly."

"Looking for me?" Holly whispered. "Or for you?"

Lisa felt her cheeks redden. "Don't be silly," she
whispered back. "He probably wants you to go home for
dinner."

They walked out into the living room and found Paul
having a lively discussion with Dave. Paul was asking him
all kinds of questions about his job. They looked up as the
girls came into the room.

"Hi." Paul greeted Lisa as if he hadn't seen her in a
long time instead of having left her an hour before.

He did a sudden doubletake when he spied Holly.
"Hey, what happened to you?"

"He noticed!" Holly grabbed Lisa's arm gleefully and
squeezed it. "Do you like it?" she asked.

"Yeah, you look terrific." He peered at her closely.
"You look a lot older."

"I am a lot older," Holly said pertly. "You're just used
to thinking of me as being twelve."

Paul laughed. "Only because you act that way. Listen,
you'd better get home. Mom's looking for you."

"Okay." Holly waved the bag of cosmetics in her
hand. "I have to go show her everything we bought. See
you later." She turned back and gave Lisa a quick hug.
"Thanks again," she said softly. "I love what you did."

She ran out of the room.

"You really are good at that." Admiration shone in Paul's eyes.

"She's very good," Dave spoke up. "Good enough to be a professional."

Lisa looked at him, surprised. She hadn't known Dave was even aware of her interest in working with makeup.

"I guess I'd better get home too," Paul said. "I'd like to talk to you again, Mr. Hubbard, about the sets, I mean. Is that okay?"

"Any time, Paul," Dave assured him. "I'll be glad to help."

"Thanks. Well." Paul edged slowly toward the front door. "I'll see you, Lisa. Bye." He left, closing the door quietly behind him.

"I'm glad you've made friends with Holly," Lisa's mother said. "The Websters seem to be a very nice family.

"Yes," Lisa said shortly. "Excuse me. I'll be in my room until dinner is ready." She knew they wanted her to stay in the living room and chat, and in a way, she would have liked it too. But they made her feel uncomfortable. She couldn't help it . . . she hoped that someday it would get easier, but at the moment she wasn't sure that would ever happen.

CHAPTER THREE

The first day of school was hot and muggy. Lisa and Holly walked together, meeting several other girls along the way. Two of them were girls Holly had introduced her to at the movies, but Lisa didn't really know them. As the conversation whirled around her, the friends catching up on their summer news, Lisa could only listen with half an ear. She was too busy concentrating on the nervous rumbling of her stomach as she anticipated the first day in this new school.

Holly went with her to homeroom and introduced Lisa to Mr. Foster, the homeroom teacher.

"I'd better get moving," Holly said, after Lisa was settled behind a desk. "My own homeroom is upstairs and I don't want to be late the first day. If I don't see you before, meet me in front of this room at twelve o'clock, and then we'll go find our lockers."

School would only be in session for half a day and Holly had already suggested that they do something together that afternoon.

As Lisa went to her shortened classes, she began to feel more assured. She had a little trouble finding some of the rooms and got completely lost going from the gym to the biology lab, but she managed to get around pretty well, and found to her delight that Holly was in her English class and her gym session.

It was exactly noon when she made her way down the main hall to Holly's locker.

"How did you make out?" Holly asked, her usual cheerful expression drawn into concern for her friend.

"Not too bad." Lisa laughed. "I only got lost twice, and most of my teachers seem to be all right."

Holly was suddenly jostled from behind by two boys coming down the hall.

"Sorry, Holly," one of them apologized. Then he took a second look at her. "Hey, what happened to you?" he exclaimed.

Lisa smiled secretly to herself. The change in Holly was really unbelievable. Lisa had worked with her for hours on the makeup instructions and they had come up with a soft, natural look that pleased both Holly's mother and themselves. But it was what Holly had done for herself that really made the change. Following Lisa's original suggestion, Holly's hair was now cut in a short swirl that framed her round face and directed attention to her fun-filled blue eyes. Even the basic shape of her face had changed—delight in her makeup-enhanced looks had sparked a desire to diet, and ten pounds had already disappeared.

"Who was that?" Lisa asked, as the two boys continued on down the hall, sending a volley of wolf whistles echoing back in their direction.

"Just two creepy friends of Paul's," Holly said, but her face flushed a bright pink and Lisa noted the tiny smile that quirked the corners of her lips.

"Hmmm . . . " Lisa raised an eyebrow. "I think there's more to this than you're telling me. What're their names?"

"The good-looking one with the brown hair is Bud Jenkins. The idiot with the black curls is Floffy Grisholm."

Lisa noted the way Holly spoke about Floffy.

"Now that school has started and Paul won't be working anymore, you'll probably see those two hanging around our house a lot," Holly went on.

Lisa tensed at the mention of Paul's name. Although she had seen him across the hedge several times in the past few weeks, he had merely smiled, waved, and gone on his way. It was almost as if the afternoon at the movies had never happened. As her friendship with Holly deepened, Lisa was more and more tempted to ask if Holly knew why Paul was avoiding her. But somehow the proper moment never presented itself, and Lisa tried to be content with listening attentively to any mention Holly made of her brother's name.

"I have a great idea," Holly said as she shoved her books in her locker and slammed the door. "Do you know how to roller-skate?"

"Sure," Lisa said, "who doesn't?"

"There's a terrific new rink in Pasadena. Let's get some of the gang together and go."

Lisa was all for it, and after Holly told a bunch of her friends the plans, a large group promised to meet them there at two o'clock. Holly and Lisa hurried home for a quick lunch of Potsy's delicious sandwiches.

"I'm going roller-skating with Holly," Lisa told the housekeeper before she ran upstairs to change her clothes.

"Tell Mom I'll try not to be too late."

"Don't worry about it," Potsy called after her. "Your mother and Dave are going out for dinner tonight."

Lisa spun around, a flash of anger flowing through her, then she caught herself and continued on up to her room. That was happening more and more lately—her mother and Dave going out to dinner together and leaving her home with Potsy. Oh, she knew that most of the dinners were business evenings for Dave, but before he had come into the picture she and her mother had always gone out to dinner together. Now it was either the three of them, or Sandra and Dave went off and left her behind. It wasn't fair, but there wasn't much she could do about it. Even Potsy, who grew closer to Lisa with every passing day, didn't want to listen to her complaints.

"Married couples have business obligations," she had said, when Lisa complained about their dining out. "And Dave is an important man in the industry."

"So why can't he go alone?" Lisa grumbled, knowing even as she said it that she was being unreasonable. "Why does Mom have to go with him?"

Potsy sighed. "I know it's hard on you, love, learning to live with a mum and dad together. You'd understand it if you had ever had your own dad around."

"My father wasn't like Dave," Lisa retorted. But deep down she knew she hadn't the slightest idea what her real father had been like.

Potsy hadn't answered her, she had just looked at Lisa with a sorrowful expression. But ever since then, Lisa noticed that Potsy always tried to tell her in advance when her mother and Dave would not be around in the evening. Lisa knew that Potsy was trying to avoid any confrontations.

Lisa had just finished zipping up her jeans when she heard the kitchen door slam and Holly say something to Potsy. She stuck some money and a comb in her back pocket and hurried out to meet her friend.

They walked up the driveway to the front of the house and Lisa snuck a look at the Websters' yard to see if Paul's car was in the driveway. It wasn't.

"Kayla is going to drive," Holly said. "I told her we would meet at her house." Kayla Morse was a friend of Holly's who lived several blocks away. Lisa had met her several times in the past few weeks, but they really hardly knew each other.

Kayla was sitting in her small Datsun waiting for them and as soon as Lisa and Holly climbed into the back seat, she gunned the motor and roared off toward the skating rink, stopping along the way to pick up two more girls.

By the time they got to the rink a crowd of almost twenty of their friends, male and female, was already assembled. Holly owned her own skates but Lisa had to rent a pair. They sat on a bench, lacing up, then took off with the crowd, circling the floor to the sound of a disco tape.

It felt good to be back on skates again. It was a sport Lisa had always enjoyed. When they had lived at the beach, before Dave's disruptive entrance into their lives, she and her mother often spent Saturday mornings skating along the path that followed the ocean shore. Indoor rink skating was a slightly different sensation, especially with the loud music blaring in the background, but it was fun with so many kids involved.

At one point Lisa noticed Bud and Floffy come in and join the rest of the skaters. Lisa watched the doorway anxiously for a few moments to see if Paul would come in too, but her vigilance went unrewarded. Paul didn't show up.

Several of the girls were skating in whip formation and Lisa watched with amusement as Floffy approached Holly, who was anchoring one end of the group. He tugged on her arm, pulling her away from the other girls, and dragged her off to skate alone with him. Holly's blue eyes gazed up at him adoringly and Lisa couldn't help giggling. She could see that her friend had a tremendous crush on Floffy, even if she did call him an idiot.

The afternoon wore on, with Lisa getting to know many of the girls in Holly's crowd on a much closer basis than she had been able to over the summer. Most of them were warm and friendly and welcomed her into the group without reservations. The only one who seemed to stand back and eye her suspiciously was Kayla Morse. Lisa shrugged to herself when she noticed. She hadn't been particularly fond of Kayla before, and if she didn't want to be friends, that was all right with Lisa.

Lisa had stopped skating for a few moments to buy an iced tea at the refreshment stand when she sighted Holly and Floffy in the middle of the floor attempting a complex dance routine. Floffy was holding a piece of paper that obviously had explicit instructions for the dance steps. As they went through the routine, Lisa could see that they didn't really know what they were doing, and were tripping and falling all over each other. It wasn't long before the other kids noticed what was going on, and soon a circle of laughing, clapping friends surrounded the two, urging them on. It was an hysterical routine, and Lisa and another girl nearby collapsed with laughter as they made their way back onto the floor to get a closer look.

The end of the routine was supposed to be a lift, but as

Floffy picked Holly up, the dance instructions slipped out of his hand and he instinctively went to grab the paper, dropping Holly onto the floor of the rink. That little maneuver got the greatest applause of all. Holly and Floffy sat sprawled on the floor, red-faced and perspiring, and laughing as hard as their friends. But as Floffy stood up and bent to lend Holly a hand in getting to her feet, Lisa saw a sudden spasm of pain flash across her face. Lisa pushed quickly through the crowd and leaned over her friend.

"What is it, Holly, what's the matter?"

Holly let out a gasp. "My leg . . . I don't know . . ."

Floffy was suddenly all concern. "What is it, Holly, did you hurt yourself?"

Holly sat numbly, nodding her head.

"Here, come over to a bench." Lisa slipped Holly's arm around her neck, trying to lift her. "I'll help you."

But Holly just sat there. "I can't, Lisa," she whispered. "I can't move."

Floffy looked frightened. "I'll carry you." He swung Holly up easily into his arms, but the sudden action must have been terribly painful, for Holly let out an uncontrollable scream. Floffy skated quickly across the room and put her gently on one of the benches. "We'll have to get her to the emergency room."

Lisa knew that she couldn't let Floffy move Holly again. "Don't do anything," she ordered. "I'm going to call her father."

"Yeah, that's right." Floffy breathed a sigh of relief. "I forgot he's a doctor."

Holly's usually healthy complexion was now an ashen gray. Several of her friends hovered around trying to console her while Lisa dashed over to the walkway surrounding the rink and yanked off her skates. She ran to the nearest pay phone, hastily shoving the coin into the slot and dialing rapidly. The phone rang for what seemed like endless moments and Lisa began to panic, afraid that no one was home. Just as she was ready to hang up she heard a click on the other end and Paul's voice came over the receiver.

"Hello."

"Paul," she gasped, "it's Lisa, Lisa Laine."

"Hi, Lisa Laine." His voice sounded warm and welcoming on the other end. "How's everything? I haven't seen you in days."

"Paul, please," she pleaded, "something's happened. We're at the skating rink, the new one in Pasadena and Holly . . . she fell . . . I mean, Floffy dropped her . . . please, Paul, she's hurt."

"Hurt?" All the warmth left Paul's voice. "Her back?"

"No," Lisa said. "It's her leg. I don't know if it's broken or not, but she seems to be in terrible pain."

"I'll be right there," Paul said. "Don't move her."

The buzz of the disconnected phone sounded in Lisa's ear and she slowly hung up the receiver. She made her way back to Holly's side, and sat down on the bench next to her friend, holding her hand.

"It's okay, Holly," she said softly. "I called Paul. He's on his way."

"Thanks, Lisa." Holly's face was drawn in pain, but her natural color seemed to be coming back into her face.

"Is it real bad?" Lisa asked.

Holly shook her head. "It doesn't hurt too much as long as I don't move."

"Good." Lisa felt relieved. "Maybe it's only a bad sprain."

Holly grinned weakly. "I hope you're right, I'd sure hate to start out the school year with a broken leg."

Lisa suddenly realized that Holly still had her skates on. "I'll take off the one on your good foot," she said, "but I think we'd better wait for Paul to see about the other one."

"Right," Floffy said. He was standing at the head of the bench, anxiously peering down at Holly. "My father isn't a doctor, but even I know you don't touch somebody if you think they have a broken bone. "When I picked her up I didn't . . ." His voice trailed off and a guilty look spread across his face.

Lisa glanced at the small gold watch on her wrist. It seemed to be taking Paul a long time to get there, but it had only been a mere five minutes since she called him. She knew that if the time was passing slowly for her, it must seem endless to her injured friend.

It was with a great sense of relief—and a small twinge of something else that she didn't have time to think about—that she finally saw Paul burst through the rink door.

He took one look at Holly's leg and let out a groan. "Sorry, babe." He patted her leg gently. "I'm not a doctor yet, but I'm pretty sure that ankle is broken." He looked worried. "We're gonna have to get that skate off before I can put you in the car, otherwise the weight of it will drag the foot down."

He looked up at his sister with gentle eyes. "I'll be as quick as I can. Lisa, you sit with her and let her hold your hand."

Lisa gritted her teeth. She had a sick feeling in the pit of her stomach, realizing this was going to be painful for her friend. She wished there was some way it could be avoided, but she knew it was impossible. She gripped Holly's hands tightly and watched over her shoulder as Paul quickly unlaced the skate.

He glanced up at Holly. "Okay?"

Holly nodded. "So far, so good," she said. "You're terrific."

"Yeah, well, I'm afraid this next part isn't going to be quite as good."

He widened the opening of the skate as far as he could and in one quick movement slipped it off her foot.

Holly let out a low moan and clutched at Lisa's hand, but seconds later she was smiling weakly. "That wasn't too bad," she murmured.

"I'm going to bind it as well as I can to try and hold it rigid until we get to the hospital," Paul said. He borrowed a long wooden spatula from the man behind the snack bar and snatched off a long silk scarf that Kayla Morse had draped around her neck.

"Hey, wait a minute," Kayla protested as he began to wrap the brightly colored silk around Holly's leg. "That's my brand-new scarf."

"I'll buy you a new one," Paul muttered without even bothering to look up, and Lisa saw the quick look of dislike that Floffy cast in the other girl's direction.

When Holly's leg was securely tied to the makeshift splint, Floffy lifted her in his arms while Paul gently balanced the injured leg in his hands.

"Okay, slowly now," he said. "Let's get her in the car."

They decided to use Floffy's old Chevy because Paul's P1800 had no real back seat. By the time Holly was settled in the automobile her face was covered with a fine sheen of perspiration. Lisa squatted on the back floor so that she could hold on to Holly's hands and keep her from moving around on the seat.

It only took a few minutes to reach the emergency entrance of the hospital. Paul dashed inside to request a gurney, and once the attendant had placed Holly on the rolling table Lisa felt herself relax for the first time in an hour.

She went into the curtained cubicle with Holly while the doctor on duty examined the injured leg. Paul went off to call his father's office and tell him about the accident.

Minutes later Holly was wheeled down to X-ray, and Lisa sat in the waiting room trying to console Floffy.

"It was all my fault." Floffy ran his fingers through his tangled curls. "I never should have tried that fancy lift."

"Don't be silly," Lisa said. "It was an accident. It could have happened to anyone."

"No." Floffy shook his head stubbornly. "It's my fault."

"It was just as much Holly's fault," Lisa assured him. "I'm sure she doesn't blame you."

"Maybe Holly doesn't," Floffy said, "but Paul sure as heck will, and Doctor Webster . . . oh, wow!" He covered his face with his hands.

Lisa couldn't help laughing. "Floffy, cut it out. It's not as if Holly is dead. She just hurt her leg, that's all. Whatever it is, it will mend."

By the time Paul rejoined them, Lisa had Floffy slightly calmed down, and when the doctor came out to report that it was definitely a broken ankle, a good clean break with no complications, all three gave an audible sigh of relief.

Within minutes, Dr. Webster came hurrying through

the emergency room door. He greeted the three of them and then went in to see Holly and consult with the doctor on duty. He emerged a short time later with a relieved look on his face.

"Nothing to worry about," he said. "She'll be in a cast for a few weeks, but she's going to be fine." He looked at Paul. "How did it happen?"

"We were skating," Lisa said, before Paul could answer. "Floffy and Holly were doing a routine in the middle of the floor and, well, I guess she landed on her foot the wrong way."

Dr. Webster shook his head. "You kids, always up to something. Well, accidents do happen to everyone. I'm just glad it wasn't anything more serious." He turned and went back into the room to be with his daughter while they were applying the plaster cast to her leg.

Floffy looked at Lisa with grateful eyes. "Thanks," he muttered. "But you didn't have to lie for me."

"I didn't lie," Lisa protested. "I told him exactly what happened."

Floffy gave a small laugh. "Not exactly. I think you forgot to mention that I picked her up and dropped her."

Paul gave a shout of laughter. "Is that what happened?"

"It wasn't funny," Floffy mumbled. "Listen, I'm gonna get out of here. I don't think Holly will want to see me after this. Just tell her I'm glad she's okay." He turned and left the room.

Lisa and Paul waited until Holly was moved to a private room where Dr. Webster wanted her kept for the night.

"I'll feel better about it if she's under professional care for twenty-four hours," he said. "She won't be able to go back to school for the rest of the week anyhow. I'll bring her home tomorrow after I do my own hospital rounds.''

"How are we going to get home?" Lisa asked as she and Paul stood outside on the steps of the hospital. "Floffy went off and left us."

"There's a bus on the corner that runs right past the rink," Paul said. "Come on, we'll go pick up my car."

When they finally settled into the P1800, Lisa looked down at her watch for the first time in hours. She was shocked to see it was almost six o'clock.

"Oh," she gasped, "Potsy must be worried sick."

"Potsy?" Paul's eyebrow went up. "What about your mother and father?"

"I told you," Lisa said grimly, "he isn't my father. Besides, my mother and Dave are going out to dinner tonight. Again," she added bitterly.

"Still haven't made the adjustment, huh?" Paul asked. "You're going to have to come to it, Lisa. I have the feeling your mother and Dave are married for good."

"Oh, I'm sure of that." Lisa knew she sounded hostile but she couldn't help it. "But in a few years it won't make any difference to me."

"What are you talking about?" Paul glanced at her curiously as he steered through the evening traffic.

"I'm almost sixteen. A couple of years more and I'll be out."

"Out?"

"Sure, out of the house," she explained, "and I won't ever have to go back."

"Are you saying you'll never see your mother again?" Paul's voice suddenly sounded very cool.

Lisa made a face at him. "Don't be silly. Of course I'll see my mother. I love her. All I meant was, I won't have to live with the two of them anymore. I'll be going to college and after that, well, my own apartment I guess. Isn't that what everybody does?''

"Sure," Paul agreed. "But I don't think everybody looks at it as getting away from their parents. You can't ever put your family behind you, Lisa.''

"I don't have a family," she said quietly. "I just have my mother. I know, you don't understand that," she went on as Paul started to protest, "but that's because you come from a different kind of home. You can't possibly understand.''

Paul shrugged. "Maybe not. Holly and my parents and I, we don't always get along, but we sure as hell always love each other—and I don't think any of us would ever want to feel that we had to put the family behind us.''

Lisa sat in silence for the rest of the way home. It was difficult trying to explain how she felt to Paul . . . that there was an intruder in their midst . . . a wedge driven between her mother and herself, a wedge that was making the break between them seem wider all the time.

Paul drove the car into the Websters' driveway and cut the engine. Their house was dark.

"Dad must have gotten ahold of Mom," Paul commented. "Her car is gone. She's probably at the hospital with Holly.''

"What will you do for dinner?" Lisa asked, the germ of an idea suddenly developing in her mind.

"I don't know, make some eggs I guess, or maybe Mom had dinner started and left in the middle.''

Tentatively, Lisa laid a hand on his arm. "Why don't you come home with me for dinner? Potsy always makes way too much.''

"Gosh, I don't know, what would your mother say?''

"I told you, Mother and Dave are going out for dinner.

I'm going to be alone. Please, Paul, come on. I know Potsy would love to have you.''

He grinned at her. "Okay, it sounds great."

They locked the car and walked around the hedge into Lisa's yard. Instead of crossing the lawn, Paul tugged her into a shadow thrown by the giant hedge.

"I want to thank you for everything you did this afternoon," he said quietly. "I know you made it a lot easier for Holly."

Lisa looked up at him with shining eyes. "And you were wonderful," she murmured. "You knew just what to do."

Paul gave a deprecating laugh. "Well, I am going to be a doctor someday too. My dad and I talk about it sometimes. I mean, I've already picked up a lot of stuff about it."

"Yes." Lisa nodded eagerly. "I could see that. You were really terrific."

His hands came up to grip her shoulders. "You're pretty terrific yourself." He leaned over and lightly brushed his mouth across hers. "I thought you were pretty terrific when I first met you."

Lisa's heart was thumping so loud she was sure he could hear it. "Th . . . thank you," she stammered. "I thought you were too. I mean, all you Websters, you're all great."

Paul laughed and grabbed her hand, tugging her across the yard toward the driveway. Just as they started over to the back door, Scruffy came bounding from around the hedge and hurtled himself against their legs. Paul picked him up and held him in his arms, scratching him affectionately under the chin.

"How about this Webster?" he asked, grinning down

43

at Lisa. "Do you think he's terrific too?"

Lisa reached out and petted the dog gently on the head. "Sure," she said, "I think Scruffy's a great old guy." And to her surprise she realized that she really meant it.

CHAPTER FOUR

Lisa tried to visit Holly every day after school. Paul brought his sister's class assignments home so she wouldn't fall behind in her school work, but Lisa brought her up-to-date on what the gang was doing and all the school gossip that Lisa could understand. Most of the names were still unfamiliar to her, but she tried to repeat it all to Holly just the way she had heard it.

On Friday afternoon she stayed late with her friend, and it was after five o'clock when she finally walked through the back door into the kitchen.

"Hello, love." Potsy greeted her with a warm smile. "Your mum's been asking for you. Where were you?"

"Sitting with Holly," Lisa said. "She's really upset that she had to miss school this week."

"Poor thing," Potsy sighed sympathetically. "Will she be going back soon?"

Lisa nodded. "On Monday if her father thinks it's okay. She'll be on crutches for a few weeks, but she should be able to get around the building." She reached for a piece of celery from a platter that Potsy was fixing.

"What did Mom want me for, do you know?"

A strange look flashed across the housekeeper's face. "They're waiting for you in the living room," she said, not really answering Lisa's question. "Don't keep them waiting now, there's a good girl."

Lisa sensed a difference in Potsy's voice, an underlying tension she didn't understand, but she merely shrugged and grabbed another piece of celery on her way to find her mother.

She found her sitting on the sofa with Dave, their fingers entwined, and they both looked up as she came into the room.

"There you are." Her mother smiled. "We've been waiting for you. Sit down, honey. Dave and I want to tell you something."

Lisa settled herself in the armchair across from them and waited expectantly. She couldn't imagine what was so important that it practically required a family conference. She could see from the looks on their faces that it couldn't be anything too serious—although there did seem to be an air of tension in the room.

She looked from one to the other. "What is it? What's the problem?"

"It's not a problem, honey." Her mother leaned forward slightly as if to touch her, but then thought better of it and settled against Dave's arm. "It's just that something very exciting has happened. At least, we hope you'll think it's as exciting as we do." She looked up at Dave as if asking for help, but he merely nodded, urging her to go on. "Lisa, I went to the doctor today and he had some wonderful news for us. We're going to have a baby!"

Lisa sat and stared at her mother. The words made no impression on her at all. She felt nothing . . . not excitement, not anger, not anything. Not once since her mother had married Dave Hubbard had the thought ever entered Lisa's head that at some time her mother might have another child.

Her mother looked at her nervously. "Lisa, aren't you going to say something?"

Lisa's mouth opened and closed. What should she say? It was as if she were detached from her own body, another Lisa standing to the side, watching the three people sitting there talking about having a new baby. What did all this have to do with her?

Dave leaned forward and said earnestly, "Lisa, we hope you'll be as happy about this as your mother and I are. After all, the baby will be your sister or brother." He smiled at her.

"I don't *need* a sister or brother." The words seemed to come from somewhere deep inside of her, and suddenly the numbness was gone and a burning rage engulfed her. How could they do this to her? Bringing another child into this house, expecting her to be excited about it, thinking she would be pleased to have a sister or a brother. It wasn't right. Why, she was a sophomore in high school and they were talking about having another child! What would her friends think? The rush of turbulent thoughts swirled through her as she inched forward and gripped the arms of her chair.

"How could you!" she gasped. "What do you want a baby for?" Tears of rage formed in her eyes and she burst forth with all the angry words and accusations that had been building inside her since she had realized the meaning of her mother's announcement.

"Lisa, please." Her mother jumped up and tried to embrace her, but Lisa angrily shoved her away.

"I can't stand it," she wailed. "You're trying to ruin my life. You did this on purpose." Even as she said the words she knew how foolish they sounded, but she couldn't seem to stop the angry tirade.

Her mother made soothing noises from above her and Lisa felt hands smoothing her hair, but Lisa pushed angrily at them, shoving them away. Suddenly Dave was standing in front of her, his hands grabbing her upper arms, shaking her slightly.

"That's enough, Lisa." The sharp edge of his voice cut through her tantrum. "Stop it immediately. You're behaving like a child."

The shock of his touching her and the coldness she sensed behind his words left her spent and sobbing quietly.

Dave returned to his seat next to her mother. "We'll have no more of that," he said sternly. "I will not have you upsetting my wife like this."

"She's my mother," Lisa said bitterly.

"Yes, she is." Dave's voice softened slightly. "And now she will be my child's mother too. I'm sorry that the thought upsets you, Lisa. But you must accept it. It's happened and it isn't going to change."

"Dave." Her mother reached out a hand toward her husband, as if pleading with him to be more sympathetic, but Dave shook his head sharply.

"I'm sorry, Sandra. This has to be settled once and for all, and right now. I will not let it fester into a major problem and upset you. I had hoped that Lisa would be happy at the news, just as we are. Obviously, that isn't going to happen, so we must settle for the next best thing—and that's for her to accept the situation." He spoke as if Lisa were not even in the room. Any guilt she'd

48

felt about upsetting her mother was now replaced by indignation at Dave and his attitude about her feelings.

Lisa stared at him resentfully, trying to think of words cutting enough to put him in his place. "I won't accept it," she declared. "And I won't accept the baby. I'll hate the baby, whatever it is. I'll . . ."

A soft sob from her mother interrupted her string of threats, and she turned to see her mother crying softly into her cupped hands. A look of concern flashed across Dave's face as he bent over Sandra to comfort her, but she jumped up from the sofa and ran from the room, the echo of her sobs trailing behind her as she fled down the hall.

Dave gave a deep sigh and pushed his fingers absently through his dark hair. "We can't go on like this, Lisa. The antagonism on your part is making all of us miserable. I don't know what I've done to earn your dislike, but I think the time has come for us to sit down and talk this over."

Lisa jumped to her feet. "I don't have to talk anything over with you. And I don't dislike you; I try not to think of you at all. Most of the time I pretend you don't even exist."

She saw the fleeting look of hurt flash across Dave's face, then his features hardened.

"You're a very sharp-tongued young lady. You weren't like this when I first met you. I'm sorry if I've been the cause of it." He stood up, weariness evident in every line of his body. "I'm sorry you feel the way you do, Lisa. Unfortunately, your attitude is making all of us unhappy. But I warn you, in the end you'll be the one to suffer the most from this." He turned and left the room, leaving her staring after him.

For a moment she stood in the empty room, then turned and raced out the front door, across the lawn to the hedge.

She wormed her way back into an overgrown area by the side of the house where the gnarled, heavy stalks had formed a natural cavelike hiding place. She leaned back against the strength of the entwined underbrush and tried to sort through the conflicting emotions threatening to engulf her.

Now that she was alone a terrible feeling of guilt began to steal through her. She hadn't meant to upset her mother like that. She hated to see her cry. But it was so unfair. Dave and her mother had seemed so happy, so elated over the news of the baby. And Lisa had only felt another pang of loss. They would be a separate family unit—her mother and Dave and their baby—and Lisa would be the outsider. How could it be any other way? Her mother would be starting over, raising her new child with a father—so different from the life that she and Lisa had had together.

Lisa's mind scurried frantically back and forth, trying to think of something to help her out of this terrible situation. School! Maybe they would send her away to boarding school. She had less than three years left, then there would be college and she would be gone for good. But Dave would have to pay for a boarding school, and she could never ask him to do that.

Maybe she could earn the money herself; maybe she could give makeup lessons or actually do the makeup for other girls. Holly was so pleased with what Lisa had done for her, and the other girls in school had all commented on it . . . but if she worked hard enough to earn the money there wouldn't be time to go to school . . . no, it was a silly idea. She was trying to pull a magic solution out of the air.

Defeated, she slumped back against the tangled undergrowth. There was no magic solution. She brushed impatiently at the drying tears on her cheeks and closed her eyes, a feeling of exhaustion coming over her.

The shock of an object landing sharply in her lap brought her upright with a start and her eyes flew open. She started to laugh at the sight of Scruffy, perched panting in her lap, eyes wide and welcoming. At the sound of Lisa's laughter, Scruffy joyously leaped up and began madly licking her cheek and nose with a wet pink tongue. Lisa grabbed the dog close and buried her face in the furry neck.

"Is this your hiding place, Scruffy?" she asked. Putting the dog down on the ground beside her, she started to scratch his neck. Scruffy squirmed with joy and flipped over on his back, paws up in the air, begging for attention. Lisa grinned and obliged, absently running her nails along the dog's belly as her thoughts returned to her own problem.

"It isn't fair, Scruffy," she said softly, repeating the thought that seemed to be uppermost in her mind. "Mom was mine, and then Dave came along, and now a new baby. Mom will be the baby's mother and Dave will be its father, and Mom will forget all about my father, and I never even saw him." Tears came to her eyes once more. "And she doesn't want to remember him and that's . . . that's not fair." Softly, she began to cry again, but this time with a feeling of terrible longing and loneliness. She wondered if she was crying for herself or for the father she never knew and the family that never was.

Scruffy seemed to sense that something was wrong, for he suddenly rolled over to his front and laid his head gently on Lisa's knee.

"I don't know what to do, Scruffy." Lisa smoothed the dog's coat with an idle hand. "I guess I have to go in and say something to Mom, but I don't know what to say. I can't tell her I'm happy for her because I'm not, and I'm not happy for me either and . . ."

"Hey, who are you talking to down there?" Paul's voice startled her and she peered out at him from her secluded nook.

"Lisa, what's the matter?" He kneeled down and pushed his way in next to her. "Have you been crying?" He ran a gentle finger along her cheek.

Lisa felt the tears well up once again.

"Hey, don't do that," he murmured. He slipped an arm around her and cuddled her head onto his shoulder. "Tell me about it, maybe I can help."

"Nobody can help." She was sobbing openly now. "It's just . . . it's just the most awful mess."

"I bet I can guess." There was a hint of amusement in Paul's voice. "You had another fight with Dave and he won."

"He won all right," Lisa said bitterly. She sniffed and tried to wipe the tears away with her hand.

Paul reached into the pocket of his jeans and handed her a tattered Kleenex. "Best I can do," he said. "I didn't know I was going to have to mop up a flood."

Lisa laughed shakily. "Thanks." She dried her cheeks and blew her nose.

"Okay, what was it about this time?" Paul asked. "Did they go to dinner again without you?"

Lisa looked down for a long moment at the damp roll of tissue in her hand. "My mother's going to have a baby," she blurted.

"A baby? Wow, no kidding! Hey, that's great." Paul suddenly stopped and looked at her. "Is that what you're upset about?"

"Of course I'm upset." Lisa looked at him angrily. "Did you think I would be excited about it?"

"Well, sure, why not?" A big grin spread across his face.

"There are lots of reasons." Lisa felt her expression close up. "I don't think I want to talk about it."

"Hey, wait." Paul reached over and put a gentle hand on her arm. "You're not worried about your mom, are you? You shouldn't be. I know she's not as young as a lot of other mothers, but honest, nowadays that's no problem. There are all kinds of tests and my dad says older mothers have nothing to worry about. I'm sure your mom will have the best care and—"

"That's not what I'm worried about," Lisa interrupted, but another pang of guilt buried itself in the back of her mind. She hadn't even thought of that aspect of her mother's pregnancy. And she should have. After all, her mother was almost forty years old. She shouldn't be having babies at that age.

"Then what's the problem? There's got to be a reason you're sitting here crying your eyes out."

"Well . . ." Lisa searched frantically for a logical reason. Somehow she couldn't just come out and say that it wasn't fair, the way she had to Scruffy. She had to have a better reason than that for Paul. "It's . . . it's embarrassing," she stammered.

Paul looked surprised. "Embarrassing? Why?" Then he gave a little laugh. "You mean . . . because your mother and Dave love each other and are going to have a baby? Lisa, I can't believe you're that old-fashioned."

"But I'm fifteen, almost sixteen. I mean, I will be sixteen when this baby comes and . . . and what will I do with it . . . I mean . . ."

"You won't have to do anything with it," Paul said persuasively. "Just love it and help your mom take care of it. Gosh, Lisa, it's going to make a big difference in your family."

Lisa stiffened at the word "family," and Paul ran a soothing hand down her back.

"Now look, you have to get over this feeling about your mother and Dave. Especially now. You must face it. You're really going to be a family. And besides"—his engaging grin appeared once more—"I think it's terrific that your mom is having a baby."

"That's because she isn't your mother," Lisa muttered.

Paul laughed. "Well, if she was my mother, I'd be just as excited. In fact, I would be even more excited."

"You can say that because you know it'll never happen." Lisa suddenly felt exhausted. "I guess there isn't any point in my going through all this, is there?" She looked up at Paul. "There isn't anything I can do about it."

"Yes there is." His voice was gentle now. "You can accept it and be happy for them and for yourself. It's going to be wonderful, Lisa," he went on earnestly, "watching a little baby grow up. And it will be your own little sister or brother."

Lisa sighed. There was no point in discussing this with Paul anymore. He could never understand the way she felt. "I guess I'd better go back in," she said reluctantly. "I'm afraid I upset my mother when she told me the big news." Again the note of bitterness crept into her voice. "I know it isn't good to get upset when you're pregnant. I'll go in and apologize."

Paul slipped out of the shrubbery and offered a hand to help her up beside him. He walked her slowly back across the lawn, an arm slung affectionately around her shoulders.

"If I were you I'd stop in the kitchen first and wash my face," he said, grinning at her.

"Oh, gosh." Lisa stopped and covered her cheeks with her hands. "I must look awful."

"Not awful, just kind of tear-stained. I think your mom would feel better if you cleaned up a little first." He gestured down the driveway. "Do you want me to come in with you?"

Lisa shook her head. "Thanks, Paul, but this isn't your problem."

"Look." He hesitated and cleared his throat. "It's going to be okay, Lisa. I promise. You'll get used to the idea. Your mom's not having this baby tomorrow, you know. It will be months before it arrives. You'll have plenty of time to get used to the idea."

"Sure." Lisa smiled slightly as if she agreed with him. "Well, I'd better go in now." She left him standing on the lawn and went off down the driveway and in the kitchen door.

Potsy took one look at her and turned away. "So they told you," she said, busying herself at the stove.

Lisa walked over to the sink and turned on the water, rinsing her face with cupped hands. "Where's Mom? Have you seen her?"

"Not since you went in there half an hour ago."

Half an hour. Was that all the time that had passed since she had come in from visiting Holly? It seemed like a week had gone by since then.

"Looks like you weren't too happy to hear the news."

Potsy looked at her without expression.

Lisa hung her head. She was beginning to feel more remorseful by the minute. Not that she felt any differently about the baby, but she wished now that she had had the strength to take the news without giving in to the emotional outburst. It was obvious from everyone's reaction that none of them understood what she was feeling. All she had done was to make a fool of herself . . . and that was the worst feeling of all.

"Excuse me," she said stiffly, "I have to find Mom. I have to . . . to tell her something."

"Lisa." Potsy stuck out a hand as if to stop her. "Don't upset her, love, it isn't good for her."

Lisa shook her head. "I won't. I'm just going to tell her I'm sorry." She tried to smile. "Listen, maybe I'm wrong and it will be terrific having a new baby around here."

All of a sudden the tears spilled over once more and Potsy pulled her into her arms, hugging her tight.

"It will be, love, you'll see. It will be."

CHAPTER FIVE

There were times over the next few weeks when Lisa felt as if she were living in the crater of a dormant volcano. Her mother had accepted her tearful apology with a grateful hug and a spate of assurances that nothing would ever change their feelings for each other. But in spite of her seeming acceptance of those assurances, Lisa knew that it wasn't really true. Things had already changed; they had started to change the day Dave Hubbard walked into their lives. Nothing would ever be the same again.

Holly's return to school had given a big boost to Lisa's spirits. Holly was in a walking cast now and able to get around in an almost normal manner. But it was impossible for her to walk back and forth from home to the campus, so Paul had been pressed into service as her chauffeur. Of course, Lisa was invited to ride along with them, which meant that every morning they crowded into the two bucket seats of the small car for the short drive. And those few minutes were the best part of Lisa's day.

Early one Saturday morning Lisa walked into the den

and found Paul and Dave squatting on the floor, critically examining what looked like a set of architect's plans. Paul looked up as she peered over their shoulders.

"Good morning." He grinned up at her. "Just getting up?"

Lisa nodded, experiencing a tingle of pleasure at seeing him so unexpectedly. "What's going on in here?"

"It's the set for the play we're doing." Paul pointed to the drawings on the floor. "The drama department is doing *Death of a Salesman* in a couple of weeks."

"And those are the sets?" Lisa asked.

"Yeah, I do most of the set designing," Paul said, "but I've got a real problem with this one." He shook his head in despair.

Dave settled back on his heels with a laugh. "Don't worry about it, we'll figure something out. It's just a matter of mechanics. Look, if you angle the main flat in this direction, instead of straight on, the way you have . . ." He worked busily with a pencil on the drawing and Paul watched his every move with avid interest.

"Is Holly up yet?" Lisa asked.

Paul looked at her absently over his shoulder. "I don't know. Could be." He turned his attention immediately back to the papers on the floor.

Lisa stood there for a few more minutes, then wandered off to the kitchen for breakfast.

"What'll it be, love?" Potsy asked. "How about some nice French toast this morning?"

"Sure, Potsy, that sounds great," Lisa answered in a dejected tone.

"What's troubling you so early in the morning?" the housekeeper wanted to know. A guarded look came over her usually cheerful face. "Haven't had words with Dave again, have you? I heard voices coming from the front of the house."

"Nothing like that," Lisa assured her. "He's in the den with Paul. They're going over some stage designs that Paul is working on."

"Designs for what?"

"Paul does most of the stage designs for the school plays," Lisa told her with a note of pride. "But I guess he's having some trouble with this new production."

"Well, he's come to the right place," Potsy said with conviction. She flipped the golden pieces of French toast expertly in the big pan in front of her. "Dave's the best there is. You just ask anyone in the business."

"I'm sure he is," Lisa murmured.

One subject she would never argue about with Potsy was the ability of Dave Hubbard. Potsy adored the man and refused to listen to anything negative about him.

Lisa drank her orange juice and finished off the French toast in a few short minutes. She didn't want to linger too long and miss Paul on his way out. But when she hurried back to the den he and Dave were still engrossed in the drawing, and Lisa could see as she peered between their heads that Dave was making extensive changes in Paul's designs.

"Now," Dave declared, settling back to take an overall look. "With the door swinging that way, you've eliminated the problem. Do you understand what I did?"

"Sure," Paul agreed readily. "I don't know why I didn't think of it myself."

Dave grinned and patted him on the shoulder. "When you've done as many of these as I have over the years, you'll see the problem without even realizing it. Actually you did a fantastic job with this, Paul. You have a real talent for it.''

Lisa could see that Paul was flattered by Dave's praise.

"Thanks. I enjoy it."

"Going to make a career out of it?" Dave asked.

"I don't think so," Paul said. "I kinda have my mind set on being a doctor. It's sort of a family tradition. Both my grandfathers and my dad are doctors and, well, I guess the next generation is up to me. I don't think Holly could make it," he added, laughing.

Dave grew serious for a moment. "Is that why you're going to do it—because the men in your family have always been doctors?"

"Oh, no," Paul hastened to assure him. "I would never do that and my dad would never make me. I'm going to be a doctor because it's what I want. This"—he gestured toward the papers on the floor—"is a lot of fun and I know I'm pretty good at it. Maybe I'll do it as a hobby." He paused. "You know, a lot of doctors do other things besides medicine. They're musicians, writers, and stuff like that. I could probably do both if I wanted."

"Sure you could," Dave agreed. "Even if you just did it for a little theater group someplace. Well"—he leaned over the drawings once again—"let's finish up with these so you can get going."

Lisa had settled herself in a big easy chair to watch them work. Now she sat up straight, listening alertly. Evidently Paul had somewhere to go after he left her house. She wondered what his plans were. She started to ask him if Holly was going with him, but he and Dave were once again absorbed in the work in front of them and Paul didn't even hear her first halting word.

Lisa slumped back into the chair. She couldn't figure Paul out. Sometimes he really seemed to like her. She had noticed that he never joked with her the way he did with some of the other girls. Instead, there was always a special look on his face when he saw her. And he seemed to smile a lot when she was around. Even his voice sounded different—more gentle and concerned—when he spoke to her.

In the beginning, Lisa had had high hopes. But in spite of this special treatment, he had never asked her for a real date. And she did know from Holly that he sometimes took Kayla Morse to a movie or to a party with his other friends. Yet when Lisa had seen him with Kayla at school he never seemed to treat her any differently than any of the other girls around.

Lisa was beginning to wonder if the only reason he was especially nice to her was because she was Holly's best friend. That would be a real disaster. The last thing she wanted was to be a substitute sister.

"I guess that about does it," Dave said a short while later, as he stood up and stretched cramped muscles. "If you have any more problems, Paul, let me know. Once the sets are finished I'll be glad to come over and check them for you if you like."

"Gee thanks, Mr. Hubbard, that would be terrific." Paul rolled up the drawings and slipped a rubber band around them. "I guess I'd better get going. Mr. Parks will wonder what's happened to me."

"And I'm about ready for my second cup of coffee." Dave smiled at them both and left the room.

"Do you and Holly have anything planned for this morning?" Paul asked.

Lisa shook her head. "She still has some work to catch

up on. Maybe we'll go to a movie this afternoon, but we haven't decided yet.'' She thought Paul was probably wondering if he had to drive them somewhere.

He stood fiddling with the roll of drawings in his hands. ''I wasn't sure if you would be interested . . . but I thought maybe . . . uh . . .'' he stuttered. ''Would you like to meet Mr. Parks?''

Lisa was bewildered. ''Who is Mr. Parks?''

''The drama teacher.'' He looked surprised. ''You mean nobody's told you about Dandy Andy?''

Lisa had heard some of the kids joking about Dandy Andy, but she hadn't known who they were talking about.

''He's great,'' Paul said. ''He used to be an actor years ago and he directed a lot of early television sitcoms, but then decided he'd rather be a teacher.'' He laughed. ''And maybe he also decided he'd rather eat regularly. Anyhow, he's terrific. Our high school is known for having the best theater department in the area, maybe even in the state. And it's all due to Dandy Andy.''

''Why do you call him that?''

''You'll see when you meet him,'' Paul said. ''He's always dressed to the teeth: shirt, tie, jacket, and classy slacks. Never jeans and a T-shirt. He's a real old-fashioned dandy. And then of course,'' he added, ''his name is Andrew. So that's how he got the name. He's always looking for good people,'' he went on soberly, ''and you're terrific with makeup. All the kids are talking about the change you made in Holly, and I've seen some of the other girls you've helped.''

Lisa felt her cheeks redden. She hadn't realized Paul paid that much attention to what she was doing.

''Are you going over there now?''

Paul glanced at his wristwatch. ''Yeah, in fact I'm late

already. They're rehearsing all day today.'' He looked at her. ''Would you like to come?''

''Sure, wait till I get my coat.''

She raced to her room and grabbed her car coat from the closet. There was no sound from her mother's bedroom across the hall. Her mother had taken to sleeping later in the morning now that she was pregnant. Lisa didn't want to disturb her in case she was still in bed, so she stuck her head through the kitchen door to tell Potsy where she was going.

When they arrived at the school auditorium, rehearsals were already in session. Paul led her down the aisle to the fourth row where Mr. Parks stood, directing the action on stage.

Paul introduced her to the teacher. ''This is the girl I was telling you about, Mr. Parks, the one who's so terrific with makeup.''

''Oh, yes, I remember. What do you think, Lisa? Would you be interested in helping us?''

Lisa looked at the nattily dressed man standing in front of her. He was exactly as Paul had described him—short and slender, with every hair combed neatly into place, his clothes color-coordinated and immaculately pressed.

''Who does the makeup now?'' she asked.

Mr. Parks shrugged. ''Most of the kids take care of it themselves. They all have some rudimentary knowledge of how it's done. I go around and check them on opening night in case there are any glaring errors. All in all, we just sort of feel our way.''

''Lisa has had some professional training,'' Paul inserted.

''Not really professional,'' Lisa protested. She went on to explain her relationship with the television crews who had helped her. She saw the look of interest grow on his face.

"Then you really do understand the finer points," he said.

Lisa nodded. "I did the makeup for a couple of plays at my old school and I do know some of the technique tricks. But remember," she hastened to add, "that was television makeup and I know it's not the same for the stage."

"That's true," Mr. Parks agreed. "TV makeup is much subtler than the stage variety, but if you know the basic techniques I don't think you should have any problems. And, in this play especially, we can use someone with expertise. Several of the characters are older and need to be properly aged. There's nothing worse than a bunch of kids with young faces and powdered hair trying to play middle-aged people. I want them to look as if they really are past their prime."

Lisa knew what he meant. She had seen amateur productions where the actors' hair had been powdered and a false mustache slapped on to connote aging. The proper way was to do it with pencil lines and color shading on the skin.

"How did you get tied up with a television crew?" Mr. Parks suddenly asked. "Is your father in the business?"

There was that question again. "My mother's husband is a set designer," she said coolly, and she felt Paul's fingers tighten unconsciously on her arm.

"Really." Mr. Parks looked interested. "What's his name?"

"Dave Hubbard."

"Oh, yes." The teacher looked somewhat surprised. "He's not just any set designer, not with his track record."

Lisa wasn't quite sure what he meant. "You mean the comedy he works on?"

"Not that thing." Mr. Parks made a dismissive motion with his hand. "I'm talking about when he was designing for the movies. He's had at least two Academy Award nominations that I know of." He looked at her strangely. "Didn't you know that?"

"No, no, I didn't," she stammered. "I guess Dave never talks about it."

"Or maybe he only talks about it to people who are interested." Paul's low voice came from behind her. "I knew about it."

Lisa spun around. "He told you?"

"When I first met him."

Lisa was taken aback. She couldn't understand why her mother or Dave had never mentioned it to her. But on second thought, it wasn't hard to figure out. When her mother had first started dating Dave, Lisa wasn't interested enough to pay any attention to who or what he was. And when they had decided to marry, her antagonism from the minute they told her about it prevented any warm sharing of confidences.

Lisa turned back to Mr. Parks, trying to think of what logical explanation she could give him for not knowing such an important thing about her mother's husband. But the teacher was watching the action on stage and Lisa realized that he had forgotten about it.

"Then I can count on you to give us a hand. All right, Lisa?" Mr. Parks glanced over at her.

"Yes, thank you, I'll be happy to give it a try."

"Come on." Paul grabbed her hand. "I'll take you backstage and show you around."

They went through a door under the stage that led up

into the backstage area. Paul showed her the sets he was constructing with the help of a crew. They were two-level, as a great deal of the action in the play took place in the son's bedroom. Paul explained some of the engineering problems involved, the reason he had wanted to consult with Dave and get his expert advise. He unrolled the plans they had worked on that morning and tacked them up on the board where his crew could also see them.

"He sure was a big help," Paul commented. "And most of the things were so simple I probably should have thought of them myself." He looked at her out of the corners of his eyes. "He's really a nice guy, Lisa. Too bad you've never let yourself get to know him."

"I know him," she said briefly and turned away. She heard Paul sigh behind her.

"Okay, I know you don't like to talk about it. Come on, I'll show you the dressing room."

There were several kids milling around and Paul told them Lisa would be helping out. Someone gave her a tattered copy of the script which had physical descriptions of the characters printed inside. Lisa sat down on a chair to study them and Paul excused himself, saying he had to get back to work on the flats.

As the cast came off the stage, Lisa sat with them and discussed their characters, making notes for what she thought would be the proper makeup. The boy playing Willy Loman, the main character in the play, would probably be the most difficult job. Turning a seventeen-year-old boy into an overweight, graying, middle-aged man, and doing it realistically, would not be easy. Lisa sketched the shape of his face and filled in his prominent features: wide-spaced eyes, full cheeks and rounded chin. She could work at home on shadings and colors.

The girl who had the role of Willy's wife would be less of a problem. It was more a matter of dressing her in the proper clothes, partially graying her hair, and judiciously applying a few lines. Lisa also knew that one way to show age in a female character was to eliminate most of the eye makeup, lending a drab appearance to the face.

The time passed quickly and Lisa could hardly believe it when Paul came to get her at three o'clock.

"Aren't you hungry?" he asked.

As soon as he said it, Lisa realized she was starved. It was hours since she had finished the two pieces of French toast, and she wondered how lunchtime could have slipped by without her even noticing it.

"Will your mom have a fit if we stop for a hamburger?" Paul asked as they walked out to the car.

Lisa laughed. "Mom won't, but Potsy will probably blow her stack. But that's okay, I'll never make it to dinner without something to tide me over."

Paul drove to the nearest drive-in and in minutes they were gorging themselves on cheeseburgers and Cokes. When he got back in the car after depositing the trash, he turned to her before starting the car.

"I'm glad you decided to help out on the play. It's a lot of work, but it's also a lot of fun."

"I know," Lisa agreed. "I always had a great time when I did it at my old school. I just wish Holly was going to be there."

"She will be," Paul said. "I thought you knew. She's one of the prompters."

"Then why wasn't she there today?"

"My mom wants her to rest as much as she can until the foot is healed. But starting Monday she'll be at every rehearsal. I thought she had told you."

Lisa shook her head. "She never said a word. I wonder why?"

Paul made a face. "She probably didn't want you to get mad at her because she wouldn't be able to spend much time with you."

"Well, now it's worked out fine. One of us won't be left alone at home."

Paul leaned a little closer. "It'll be nice to see you more often." He reached out and ran a finger gently down her cheek. "I'm sorry I haven't been there for you as much as I would have liked the last couple of weeks. I know you needed somebody, but I had to get those sets started."

Lisa felt a flood of relief. He *had* wanted to be with her. But being Paul he had to fulfill his obligation to the drama department.

"I know how upset you were," he was saying. "But I didn't want to talk about it in front of Holly on the way to school. I wasn't sure how much you told her."

"Not much," Lisa admitted. "I guess I realized that I overreacted to the news. It was bad enough that *you* saw me like that. I didn't want to inflict it on Holly too."

"Hey, come on." He lifted her chin so that he could look directly into her eyes. "I can understand why you took the news that way. I'm sure it was a shock. But I knew once you really thought about it you'd see that it was really terrific."

Lisa didn't answer him. She had acted like a big enough fool in front of him. She wasn't going to tell him that she hadn't changed her mind about the baby, she had simply come to understand that there wasn't a thing she could do about it. She could only swallow her unhappiness.

Paul settled back behind the wheel and started the car, driving slowly home. After parking in his driveway, he turned to her once again.

"Are your folks going out tonight?"

This time Lisa didn't correct him when he referred to her mother and Dave that way. "I'm not sure," she said. "But it's Saturday night and they usually go somewhere."

"Then you're going to be home alone . . . or is Potsy staying?"

"Don't be silly." She laughed at him. "I'm not a child. I don't need a babysitter. Potsy goes to her own apartment at night."

"Well, listen." He played with the car keys in his hand. "I'm not doing anything. How about if I come over and we play some records or something?"

"Sure, that would be great," Lisa said, trying not to shout with joy. A sudden brilliant idea struck her. "Do you know if Floffy Grisholm is doing anything tonight?"

Paul looked at her as if he didn't understand. "I have no idea, why?"

"I thought it might be fun if we asked him, and maybe Holly could come too."

Paul leaned back and let out a shout of laughter. "Are you matchmaking, Lisa?"

"I don't know what you're talking about," she protested.

He grabbed her hand and squeezed it. "Yes you do— I've noticed that budding romance too. I just wasn't sure if anybody else had."

Eagerly she squeezed his hand. "The day Holly broke her ankle, I could tell."

"So could I," Paul agreed. "Terrific idea. Come on." He opened the car door. "I'll call Floffy and if he says okay, we'll tell Holly."

Lisa followed him into the Websters' house, feeling happier than she had in weeks. Paul had asked to spend the evening with her, and Holly and Floffy would get together at last. The only cloud on her horizon was her problem at home. But there wasn't anything she could do about that. For tonight, at least, she would shove it aside and enjoy the time with Paul.

CHAPTER SIX

Lisa spent all of her spare time that next week poring over books on theater makeup. Her feelings about Mom and Dave and the new baby were set aside as she became absorbed in the challenge of her new "career." She realized after a few days that Paul was right . . . the baby wasn't expected for months yet. She had plenty of time to come to terms with the problem.

She was even able to thank Dave with honest sincerity when he brought home two professional books on makeup he had borrowed for her from a friend at the studio. The fleeting thought that he had probably done it to make points with her still didn't take away from the fact that she appreciated the help.

By the evening of dress rehearsal, Lisa had everything worked out on paper. She had experimented with lines and shadings on the four actors playing the lead roles. The two teenage boys were easy. Aside from a coating of pancake makeup and some highlighting on their eyes, there wasn't much she had to do to them. But the two older characters were a real challenge. When she'd finished she was extremely pleased with the results.

So was Dandy Andy. Just before the final rehearsal began, he went backstage to find her, asking her to sit with him for a few minutes during the first act so that they could make any changes in the makeup that might be needed.

"But I don't think there will be anything major," he said as he scrutinized the two leads. "You've done a fantastic job, Lisa, as good as any professional I've ever seen."

Lisa felt a swelling of pride. It was one thing for her to be satisfied with her work; Mr. Parks's approval was the important thing.

The first hint of disaster came early in the opening scene. One of the things Lisa had done to age the boy playing Willy Loman was to thicken his eyebrows with artificial hair. As the play progressed, Lisa noticed that the actor kept dabbing at his left brow. Either she hadn't applied enough glue, or the hot lights and greasy makeup kept it from sticking. Finally, the offending piece came off in the boy's hand and he shoved it impatiently into his pocket, causing a titter of laughter to run through the few spectators in the almost empty auditorium.

"Can't have that," Mr. Parks muttered to her out of the side of his mouth.

"I'll see to it," Lisa whispered—and she would, even if she had to put a whole bottle of glue on it.

But the incident with the makeup was only the start of an evening of disasters. The first time one of the characters sat down on the side of a bed on the second level of the scenery, the legs gave way and the actor found himself sitting on the floor, a look of total bewilderment on his face. The whole cast broke up over that one, and it wasn't until Mr. Parks became really angry that they were able to control their giggles and get back to the play.

But the serious disaster happened in the second act when one of the flats suddenly collapsed. The few people watching in the auditorium seats rushed up on the stage to make sure no one had been hurt. Lisa found Paul backstage vigorously swearing to himself.

"It's my fault," he said fiercely. "I should have known this would happen."

"It's not your fault," Lisa said. "It's Dave's fault. I saw his drawings for this flat."

Paul shook his head. "No, it was me. I thought Dave's system was too complicated. It was faster and easier to do it my way, but he knew what he was talking about. I should have listened to him."

The stage crew had hastily removed the damaged flat so that they could get on with the rehearsal.

"Have that thing fixed by tomorrow afternoon," Mr. Parks said briefly to Paul. "I don't care if you have to stay up all night."

"Yes, sir, it's no problem," Paul assured him. "I know exactly what to do."

"Then why didn't you do it the first time?" Mr. Parks muttered as he walked down the stage steps to his seat in the auditorium.

"Dandy's got his dander up," one of the stage crew whispered.

"Yeah, but he has a right to be sore," Paul admitted. "If I had done it right the first time, this wouldn't have happened. I'm just glad no one got hurt."

Lisa returned to her seat next to the drama teacher as the rehearsal picked up from where the accident had happened. Things seemed to go from bad to worse. The actors stumbled over their lines and at one point Holly, who was the main prompter, had to limp out onstage to give one of the actors his cue; he couldn't seem to hear her whisper from backstage.

Mr. Parks threw his hands in the air in despair. "Oh, that's terrific," he yelled. "Are you going to do that tomorrow night? I don't think the audience will appreciate it if the prompter comes strolling out onstage."

Once again the cast and spectators started to laugh, but this time it was from nervous tension and the realization that they were doing a lousy job. Dandy Andy was usually a pretty easygoing guy, but they all knew the kind of temper he had when things went wrong. And they couldn't get much worse than they were now.

He let them struggle through to the end of the play before he ripped into them, tearing their performances apart, criticizing moves and delivery and the quality of performance.

When he finally dismissed the cast, Lisa and Holly hung around to help Paul and the stage crew with the repairs on the offending flat. It was simply a matter of rearranging the braces behind the scene and they were finished with it before midnight.

It had started to rain and Paul dashed to the school parking lot to get the car while the girls waited inside.

On the way home they huddled together, damp and sleepy, each of them in a miserable mood. Lisa couldn't forget about the offending eyebrows, and she was sure Paul was thinking about his mistake, as Holly was about her unexpected appearance on the stage.

"Tomorrow night is going to be a disaster," Lisa moaned. "And there isn't even time for another rehearsal."

"I don't think another rehearsal would help," Holly said bluntly. "None of them knew their lines tonight. When Steve said he couldn't hear me prompting him, what else was I supposed to do? I had to come out onstage."

"Well, you'd better not do it tomorrow night," Paul declared. "Dandy is liable to kill you."

The memory of the teacher's furious reaction to Holly's surprise entrance suddenly got them giggling, and as Paul turned into the driveway the three of them were hysterical with laughter. Finally they calmed down, trying to catch their breaths.

"We're so exhausted, we're getting crazy," Paul said. "We could all use a good night's sleep."

"You think this was bad, wait till tomorrow night," Holly said. "That's when we get to make fools of ourselves in front of an audience."

They all moaned in unison, and dragged themselves home, each worrying about what might happen opening night.

But all their worries were in vain. In that magical way of the theater, opening night was a smashing success. The scenery drew murmurs of appreciation from the audience. The actors remembered all their lines and performed with marvelous precision. And Lisa's makeup job drew some complimentary comments.

When the performance was over and the auditorium had emptied, Dandy Andy gathered the cast and crew around him on the stage to compliment them and tell them how proud he was of their work. There was another performance the following night and two more the next weekend, but after the way things had gone that evening, everyone knew they had nothing to worry about.

Most of the cast and crew arranged to meet at the local hamburger place as soon as makeup had been removed, costumes hung up in readiness for the next performance, and the stage set for the opening scene the following evening.

Lisa had finally managed to find Paul in the milling crowd backstage when Holly came limping over to announce breathlessly that she was going to ride with Floffy Grisholm. Floffy was working as part of Paul's stage crew, and Lisa had noticed several times over the past few weeks that Holly and Floffy seemed to gravitate toward each other when they were backstage. In fact, since the evening the four of them had spent listening to records and dancing at Lisa's house, the romance between Holly and Floffy seemed well underway. They weren't going steady yet, but Lisa was sure it wouldn't be long before the two of them devoted all of their social time to each other.

She wondered if that time would ever come for her and Paul. Holly hadn't said anything recently about his dating Kayla Morse, but that could mean Holly simply didn't want to upset her. There were many evenings when Lisa knew Paul's car was missing from the driveway next door, and she wondered if he was out with his friends or seeing Kayla.

As she slid into the bucket seat of his car, she thought how nice it was to be alone with Paul for a change, not cramped into the small space with Holly beside her. And how wonderful that Kayla was not a member of the cast or crew and had had no reason to see Paul during rehearsals, especially the last two weeks when everyone's attention had been focused on the production.

By the time they got to the restaurant the place was

jammed. They managed to squeeze in two more chairs around the table where Holly and Floffy were already downing their food. Paul ordered cheeseburgers for Lisa and himself and when they arrived, hot and juicy with cheese oozing out the sides, Lisa bit hungrily into hers, relishing every mouthful. Nervously anticipating the performance, she had barely been able to eat any dinner that evening. Now she felt completely relaxed, and when she had finished eating she sat back contentedly, sipping the iced tea in her glass. The loud chatter around her was all about the play, and because it was Friday night none of the kids were anxious to hurry home. Most of the cast planned to sleep late in the morning and take it easy during the day until it was time to return once again to the auditorium.

But finally a few of them began to drift away, and as the crowd thinned out, Holly moved around the table to claim an empty chair next to Lisa.

"It was super, wasn't it?" She was enthusiastic. "Everybody did just great, and the makeup was perfect. I heard a couple of people talking in the lobby afterwards about how natural it looked. Dave was right, you are good enough to be a professional."

At the mention of Dave's name, Lisa sniffed with disdain. "What does he know?" she said. "I probably wouldn't even like being a professional makeup artist."

For the first time since they had become friends, Holly really looked annoyed with her. "You'd be determined not to like it just to get even with Dave, wouldn't you? You'd do anything to cross him."

Lisa was taken aback. "That isn't so."

"Oh, yes it is," Holly said fiercely. "Paul told me how upset you are about what's going on in your house and frankly, Lisa, I think you're crazy.''

Lisa's first reaction was one of hurt that Paul had discussed her with his sister. But then she realized that since Holly was her best friend, Paul had probably assumed she had told Holly all about it. But she hadn't. Aside from the few times Paul had brought it up in their conversation, Lisa hadn't told anyone. She simply wanted to forget about it.

''I have plenty of time to decide what I'm going to be.'' She tossed her head back. ''As a matter of fact, I'm seriously considering becoming a doctor. I have the grades for it and . . .''

Holly started to laugh. ''And Paul's going to be a doctor.''

Lisa leaned forward and glared at her. ''That isn't the reason. I thought about it long before I ever met Paul.''

''Oh, Lisa, come on. You know that isn't true,'' Holly protested, still grinning.

But Lisa was really angry now—angry that Holly didn't believe her and doubly angry because Holly was right! She hadn't ever thought of medicine as a career until she'd met Paul Webster. In fact, she hadn't even thought about it until five minutes ago when Holly brought up the subject of Dave and the makeup. But now that she had declared her intention she was going to defend it fiercely until Holly believed her.

The subject wasn't mentioned again that night. All the following week Lisa waited to see if Holly had said anything to Paul, but evidently she hadn't; Lisa was sure he would have said something about her intent to study medicine.

The two performances the following weekend were

both well-accepted. After the final one on Saturday evening, the cast and crew and their dates gathered at the home of the boy who had played the part of Willy Loman for the big cast party. It was a tradition at the school for one of the leading players to play host for the event.

The party was held in a basement recreation room. A crush of bodies jammed into the small area for dancing or hung around the huge table laden with food. It soon became unbearably warm.

"Let's get out of here for a few minutes," Paul said, tugging at Lisa's hand. "I feel like I'm going to melt."

They grabbed their jackets and ran up the basement stairs, going out the front door to stroll idly up and down the sidewalk in front of the house. Paul draped his arm casually across her shoulders as they sauntered back and forth.

"Mmmm," he said, looking up at the darkened sky and sniffing the night air. "Smells as if somebody has a fire going in their fireplace. I guess summer is really over at last."

"I should think so." Lisa laughed. "It's Halloween next week."

"Sure, I know," Paul said. "But this is California. Two years ago, I remember we went to the beach on Thanksgiving Day."

"But that's unusual," Lisa demurred. "You have to admit that doesn't happen every year."

"And I guess this won't be that kind of a year," Paul agreed. "There's a definite snap of autumn to the air."

"Do you ever wish you lived someplace where they get snow?" she wondered.

"No way," Paul said. "When I want to ski I just drive

up to the mountains. I'm very happy to live where it's warm and sunny most of the time. That's the only thing I don't like about New Year's Day." He shivered.

Lisa looked at him, perplexed. "What are you talking about?"

"The Rose Parade," he said. "What did you think I meant?"

Lisa stopped and put her hands on her hips. "Paul Webster, you're talking in riddles. Would you please explain what you mean?"

"Gosh, I forgot." He shook his head. "You haven't lived here long enough to know. Our town enters a float in the parade every other year. And I've helped with it the last couple of times."

"You build the float?" Lisa was astounded.

"Not the whole thing," Paul said, laughing. "The basic frame is built by professional float makers. But there's lots to do once it's delivered to us and . . . hey!" He stopped and clapped a hand to his forehead. "I've just had a fantastic idea! The motif this year is a Japanese tea garden. How would you like to help with the girls' makeup?"

"What girls?"

"We're having four girls on the float," he explained. "They're going to be dressed in Japanese costumes. And they're going to need some special makeup." He moved around her excitedly. "It's a fantastic day, Lisa. You'll have to get up at three o'clock in the morning and meet at the Tournament of Roses headquarters in Pasadena. Around seven o'clock in the morning the people riding the floats climb on and they have to stay there until the parade ends around eleven. If you came down, you'd be a big help. Do you think you'd like to do that?''

"Sounds marvelous," she said. "What do you do?''

"I'll be starting days ahead of time helping to decorate the float. The city of Pasadena has several special warehouses where we do that before the floats are trucked over to Orange Grove Avenue. By the last couple of days we're working night and day. The fresh flowers have to be put on at the last possible moment so they don't wilt and die. They fly flowers in from all over the world for the parade.''

"How do they choose the girls for the float?" Lisa was curious.

"There's a contest at the high school. A special committee picks them. The contest is next month sometime.'' He looked at her closely. "Why, do you want to enter?''

"Not me." Lisa shook her head. "I'd much rather work with you. I mean, on the makeup . . .''

He stopped in the middle of the sidewalk and turned to face her. He was suddenly serious. "I'd like to have you there helping out, Lisa. I like it when you're near me.''

Lisa felt her heart leap with joy.

"But there's one thing you have to understand," he went on. "I'm going to be real busy once we start decorating the float. There won't be time for fooling around or anything.''

"Fooling around?" Lisa questioned.

He grinned down at her. "Yeah, you know, like this.''

And suddenly his arms were tight around her and he was pulling her close to his chest. He bent his head and then his lips were touching hers, lightly at first, then with a strength and intent that let her know how strong his feelings really were for her.

When he finally lifted his head they stared at each other for a long moment. Then Lisa began to smile. She couldn't help herself, she was so happy.

Paul grinned at her in return. "That was nice." His voice held a note of satisfaction. "I've been wanting to really kiss you for a long time."

"Then why did you wait so long?" she asked softly.

He made an offhand gesture. "I figured I'd wait until the right moment came along." His voice lowered. "And that was the right moment."

Before she could answer, he bent over her once again and kissed her with loving warmth. "Your cheeks are cold," he said as he held her in a tight embrace. "Come on, let's go back inside." He tucked her arm through his and they walked slowly back to the front door of the house.

"Do I have to speak to someone about working on the float?" she asked.

"There's a committee meeting next week," Paul said. "I'll take you over that night and you can volunteer. It's no big deal. You just sign up for it. They're glad to have anybody who is willing to work. But remember," he cautioned, "it's very hectic and takes a lot of time."

She looked at him teasingly. "Are you telling me that you won't have room in your life for me?"

But when he answered he was deadly serious. "You always have room in your life for the people you love, Lisa. I think you need to understand that."

She knew immediately what he was referring to. But she refused to let any of her family problems intrude on the happiness she was feeling tonight.

"Come on." She grabbed his hand and tugged him toward the basement stairs. "The food's probably all gone by now and if I know you, you're starving."

He fell in with her mood immediately. "The food!" he cried. "How could I have forgotten that?" He raced down the basement stairs, pulling her along behind him.

CHAPTER SEVEN

Holly's cast was removed the following week.

"Mom made me promise that I'd skip the skating for a while," she said with a mock groan as she displayed the newly naked ankle to Lisa. "But I guess we can find other things to keep us busy."

"I'm sure we'll think of something," Lisa said dryly. "Uh, now that we can walk again, I guess Paul won't be taking us to school anymore?" Her voice ended on a questioning note and Holly's eyes glinted with laughter.

"Well, *I* may be walking, but I know Paul will be happy to take you since you've probably forgotten how."

"Don't be silly," Lisa said, flustered. "I was just wondering . . ."

"I'm teasing you." Holly's look softened. "Of course you should go with Paul—you're his girlfriend, aren't you?"

"I don't know if I am," Lisa admitted. "What about Kayla?"

"What about her?" Holly countered. "I happen to

know for a fact that Paul hasn't taken her out in weeks. Not since before the play.''

Lisa felt a tremendous sense of relief. She had wondered if Paul managed to find time in his busy schedule to see the other girl. And since the end of the play, a week ago, he had been coming over to Lisa's house much more frequently. She had sensed a shift in their relationship since the night of the cast party. Every night before she fell asleep she thought back again to the walk they had taken in the cool October night.

This weekend was Halloween and Paul had asked her to go with him to a party at a friend's house. Holly and Floffy were going with them. Lisa had been trying to persuade herself that his asking her meant he was no longer interested in Kayla Morse, but hearing Holly say the words out loud was a tremendous reassurance. After all, Holly was his sister and they were very close. Lisa was sure Paul didn't confide all of his secrets to Holly, but he must have said something to her about how he felt.

Lisa had come up with a great idea for a costume for the party, and Paul and Potsy had both helped her work it out. The idea had come to her while reading an article in a magazine about the artist Andy Warhol; she suddenly decided to go as a Campbell's Soup can.

Paul fixed up a wire frame that slipped over her head and rested on her shoulders. Potsy helped her cover it with plastic and encase it in heavy drawing paper. Painting the label on had taken many hours of painstaking work, but as she got ready the night of the party she knew it was a sensational costume.

She walked carefully into the den to show her mother and Dave, prepared for their outburst of laughter, knowing it would be meant in a complimentary way. She turned slowly so they could get the full effect of the soup can design. She had to move carefully as the wire frame tended to dip right and left, making her movements awkward.

"Lisa, it's fantastic!" her mother exclaimed. "It was worth all the time and effort. You're going to be the hit of the party. We'll have to store it away carefully tomorrow so that you can use it again sometime."

"Hey, I have an idea," Dave said teasingly. "Maybe Lisa will lend it to you now that you're growing out of all your clothes." He leaned over and patted her front affectionately.

"No!" Lisa hissed, her temper suddenly wildly out of control. "If my mother is fat and ugly and clumsy, it's your fault! You did it to her! She didn't want another baby, it was all your idea. She . . ."

Lisa's voice faltered as her mother stood up slowly, her face drawn in pain. She stood silently for an endless moment, tears trickling slowly down her ashen cheeks. Without saying a word she turned and left the room, her movements slow and defeated.

Lisa stared at the empty doorway, her costume hampering her from running after her mother. She spun around, almost toppling over as Dave spoke behind her.

The expression on his face was cold and forbidding, and Lisa felt a small shiver of fear. He had never looked at her that way before.

"We've got to settle this, Lisa," he said. "I cannot permit you to upset your mother this way any longer. I've tried to get along with you ever since your mother and I got married, but there doesn't seem to be any use in trying any longer. No matter what I do, you refuse to cooperate."

A sudden look of defeat came over him and he rubbed

absently at his forehead. "I'm sorry you feel the way you do . . . I had really hoped . . ." He sighed and leaned heavily against the back of the chair. "We must come to an understanding, Lisa, a way we can live together without constant antagonism. We both love your mother and this continual friction between us is making her very unhappy."

Lisa found herself swallowing in huge gulps. Dave's words seemed to come at her from a great distance and she felt herself frowning as if trying to make sense out of the strange phrases.

"I'm laying down the ground rules now," he went on, once again standing erect and speaking in that cold, level tone. "You can say anything you want to me in private, or you can refuse to talk to me altogether if that's what you wish. But you will not make any more biting remarks in front of my wife. Do you understand?"

"Sure, I understand." Lisa's voice sounded high and shrill even to her own ears. "You want me to lie or play games or—"

A heavy flush suffused Dave's face and Lisa could see that he was having difficulty controlling his anger. "I don't ever want you to lie, Lisa. I would never ask that of you."

"Oh, really," she taunted. "Then what are you asking me? You tell me not to say anything in front of my mother, you say . . ."

Paul's voice cut through her words as he walked jovially into the room. "Hey, Lisa, turn around. Let me see how it came out." His glance slid across the room. Dave tried to give him a welcoming smile, but he couldn't hide the whiteness of his knuckles where his hands gripped the back of the chair.

Lisa wondered how much, if anything, Paul had heard of their argument, but he seemed to be his usual cheerful self. She breathed a sigh of relief. He had come in at the opportune moment. She didn't want to get into a knock-down, drag-out, verbal battle with Dave. He knew how she felt about him. There was no point in losing control of herself the way she had been doing.

Paul looked over at the clock on the mantelpiece. "We'd better get going or we'll be late." He looked around. "Are you going to wear a coat?" He laughed as his glance settled on her once more. "On second thought, you'll never get into a coat."

"I'm wearing my mother's cape," Lisa said. "It's out in the hall."

Paul said goodnight to Dave and Lisa started to follow him out of the room, but Dave's voice stopped her.

"I meant what I said, Lisa." His voice was now low and controlled. "In the future, when you have something to say to me, please say it in private."

Lisa looked back at him over her shoulder. "And if I don't?"

"Then we'll have to make other arrangements." There was no hesitation on Dave's part. "I will not permit my wife to be upset like this any longer."

Lisa turned without answering him and maneuvered her way out of the room as quickly as she could. Paul was waiting for her in the hall, her mother's cape held wide. He slipped it over her shoulders and ushered her out.

The party was going full blast when they arrived and Lisa's costume was a sensation, just as she had hoped. She won the prize for originality, and all evening long kids came up to her to tell her how terrific they thought she looked.

But as great a party as it was, and with all the fun everyone else was having, Lisa never really got into the mood of the evening. She kept telling herself that her fight with Dave had taken the edge off her pleasure. But deep down she knew that wasn't really what had upset her; it was the memory of her mother's face when she'd left the room in tears. Knowing she had hurt her mother deeply, Lisa was torn between a guilty feeling of satisfaction that her mother was getting what she deserved, and the knowledge that she didn't want to hurt her in any way—for any reason—because she loved her more than anyone else in the world.

Paul's behavior toward her seemed to be perfectly normal. He was always at her side, laughing as they tried to dance with the soup can between them, stealing a quick kiss as they were bobbing for apples, holding her hand most of the evening when it became obvious it was impossible to put an arm around her shoulders.

On the way home in the car they laughed and talked about the party they had just left, but when Paul pulled into his driveway and turned off the ignition he suddenly turned serious.

"I guess things aren't going so well over at your place, are they?" He stretched his arm casually along the back of the seat.

Lisa's pleasure in the evening quickly faded. "How much did you hear?" she asked, knowing that had to be behind his question.

Paul shrugged. "I'm not sure, but most of it, I guess."

"Did you see my mom?" she wanted to know.

Paul nodded. "But I don't think she saw me. She was headed for the kitchen, but I could see that she was crying, and when I got to the living room door I heard Dave's voice."

"Yelling at me," Lisa put in angrily.

Paul shook his head. "He wasn't yelling, Lisa. He was upset. But I thought he was being pretty level-headed about it."

Her eyes shot up to stare at him intently through the dark. "What are you trying to say?"

Paul turned away from her slightly and stared blankly through the windshield. "I'm saying I think Dave was right; you're being unreasonable, Lisa. Dave is concerned about your mother's health, emotional and physical."

"And you think I'm not," she said bitterly.

He turned to her with an expression of regret. "I know you're not. You wouldn't be acting this way if you were thinking about her."

Lisa's eyes filled with tears, and she tried desperately to blink them away. But it was no use; in seconds they were streaming down her cheeks. Paul made a soft sound of protest as he leaned over to brush them away, but she slapped his hand away from her face, giving in to her unhappiness with hysterical vehemence.

"What do you know about it?" she cried. "It isn't your mother who's having the baby . . . and you have a father and you have Holly . . . and Scruffy . . . and . . . and I have no one." She covered her face with her hands, trying to stifle her loud sobbing.

"That isn't true," Paul said in a pleading tone. "You have your mom and Potsy and Holly and me. And you'd even have Dave if you'd only change your attitude about him."

"Stop saying that!" she screamed at him.

91

He grabbed her shoulders, trying to tug her close to his chest, but the frame of the soup can proved to be an insurmountable barrier.

"Take that damn costume off," he said between gritted teeth as he yanked at the wires.

"I . . . I can't," she sobbed.

"Why not?"

"Be . . . because I only have a leotard on underneath."

Paul gave a strangled laugh. "Don't worry about it. You can put your mom's cape around you. Come on, I've seen a girl in a leotard before."

He helped her wrestle the clumsy costume over her head before gently draping the voluminous cape around her shoulders. She wrapped it around her legs and settled back into the coziness of its woolen warmth.

This time when Paul took her in his arms she leaned against him with a grateful sigh.

"Now let's get back to our discussion." His voice sounded determined.

Lisa felt calmer now. She pushed her hands through the openings in the cape and folded them quietly in her lap.

"It's true, what I said." Her voice was calm and reasonable. "You get along with your parents, and you have Holly and Scruffy besides."

Paul started to speak, but she held up her hand to stop him.

"I know that you and Holly and Potsy are my friends, but it isn't the same thing. I used to have my mom but she belongs to Dave now. And when the baby comes, they're going to be a whole new family. Can't you see that?" She looked up at him with pleading eyes.

"You're wrong," he said softly, touching her wet cheek with a gentle finger. "I know you have this crazy fantasy about our family being perfect—but it isn't true, Lisa, honest. Holly and I fight, and we both have arguments with my mom and dad, and they have arguments too. Every family does." He gave a small laugh. "I guess about the only one in our house who gets along with everybody all the time is Scruffy." He tweaked her chin teasingly. "And you don't even like Scruffy."

She turned on him, annoyed. "I do so like Scruffy. Don't tell me who I like."

Paul threw back his head and laughed. "See, you *can* change your mind about somebody . . . or something. Or do you only change your mind about dogs?" His arm tightened around her. "I just want to say one more thing to you, Lisa, and I don't want you to get angry at me. I promise after this I'll stay out of it because I know it really isn't my business. But you know I care about you and maybe what I have to say will help."

She stared down at her folded hands and nodded. "Go ahead, say whatever you want." She straightened up on the seat, moving out of his grasp.

Paul accepted her detachment and turned to grip the steering wheel with tight fingers. "You told me when you first moved here that you had nothing against Dave personally, you just didn't like his being married to your mother." He glanced over at her. "Is that still true?"

Lisa nodded without answering.

"Well, I have to tell you." Paul let go of the wheel and leaned back against the car seat. "I've gotten to know Dave pretty well since then and he's really a terrific guy. He loves your mother. Anybody can see that they're very happy together." He half turned toward her. "Except for the problem with you. You're the one who's making the trouble, Lisa, not them."

Lisa felt as if she couldn't breathe. The hurt she felt at Paul's words was almost unbearable. And the worst part was she knew he was right. But knowing it didn't make her feel any better, and it didn't help her with her feelings of loss and betrayal.

Endless moments of silence surrounded them, then Paul slid across the seat and pulled her gently back into his arms.

"I'm sorry," he muttered. "I shouldn't have said that."

"It's all right," she assured him in a low voice. "You're probably right." She looked up at him. "And I'll think about what you said. But I don't want to talk about it anymore, Paul, not tonight."

"Sure." He leaned over and kissed her lightly on the cheek.

She was suddenly seized with a fierce longing for someone to hold her tight and she twisted around, flinging her arms around his neck, and raised her mouth to his. He seemed to understand her need, returning her kiss with equal fervor before holding her gently away from him.

"It's getting late," he said quietly. "I'd better take you home." He came around to open her car door, helping her wrestle the clumsy costume out of the back seat where they had tossed it earlier.

They walked across the lawn, damp now from the heavy night moisture. Lisa put her key in the front door lock then turned to Paul for a last good night. He kissed her gently once again and cupped her face for a moment in his hands.

"Sleep tight and don't worry, everything's going to be fine," he murmured with a reassuring smile.

But Lisa could see the look of pity buried deep in his eyes and she knew that something had changed between them tonight. Paul felt sorry for her, but that didn't change his belief that she was wrong. She was afraid that he would never feel quite the same about her again.

CHAPTER EIGHT

By the time Lisa's sixteenth birthday rolled around she had made so many new friends and had been invited to so many parties and get-togethers that her mother felt it was time they did some reciprocating. This year Lisa's birthday happened to fall on the Friday after Thanksgiving. Since everyone was out of school for the long holiday weekend, they decided to celebrate the important event with a five o'clock backyard barbecue.

The weather turned out to be very cooperative. The day was warm and sunny, and when the guests started arriving in the late afternoon the air was still comfortable, almost like Indian summer.

Paul and Holly were the first to arrive, and Lisa experienced a feeling of self-satisfaction as she watched her friend walk down the driveway toward her. Holly's transformation was now complete. She had lost another ten pounds, reaching the goal of her desired weight. Ever since Lisa had suggested a new hairstyle, Holly had been experimenting with different cuts and sets. Tonight she appeared with still another style: this time the ends of her shorter-length blond hair were turned under in a neat pageboy. Now that her full cheeks had narrowed into slim planes, the new hairstyle was extremely flattering. When Floffy appeared on the scene a few minutes later, Lisa wasn't surprised to see him make a beeline straight for Holly. That romance was progressing nicely and Lisa gave herself an imaginary pat on the back for her part in getting them together.

By five-thirty the backyard was swarming with her friends, male and female. Potsy appeared from the kitchen bearing huge bowls of chili and green salad, while Dave manned the gas barbecue, tending juicy hamburgers and hot dogs that were gobbled up as fast as he cooked them. Eager fingers grabbed slices of hot garlic toast from baskets at each end of the serving table, and for a while there was only a low murmur of conversation as everybody settled down on the lawn with plates in their laps to enjoy the terrific spread Potsy had produced in honor of the occasion.

By the time everyone had finished eating, the serving table looked as if a tornado had whirled across it. There was barely enough left to make it worthwhile carrying back to the kitchen.

Lisa ducked into the house to give Potsy a big hug and thank her.

"Everybody loved it," she said. "You're the greatest cook ever."

Potsy beamed at her with pleasure. "Thank you, love, but you go on outside now." She shooed her out the door with her apron. "We aren't finished yet."

Lisa grinned and ran back outside. She knew there had to be a birthday cake coming up next and when she got back out in the yard she found the serving table completely cleared off and waiting. In a few moments Dave appeared carrying a huge sheet cake iced with chocolate and decorated with pink rosebuds and "Happy 16th Birthday Lisa" written out in white icing. There were sixteen pink candles on the cake and one big white one in the corner "to grow on." Everyone sang "Happy Birthday" as Lisa blew out the candles and made a wish.

As she picked up the knife to cut the first piece, she felt Paul slip his arm around her waist and give her a quick squeeze. She looked up to smile at him, and happened to glance across the table where her mother and Dave were standing ready to help serve the cake. For a moment Lisa was taken aback. The look of love and pride on her mother's face was echoed in identical fashion on Dave's features. Once again Lisa felt a momentary stab of guilt and remorse. A traitorous thought flashed through her mind. Why couldn't Dave have been her real father? Then none of this turmoil would have happened. She would have been free to love him, and her feelings about the new baby . . . .

The fleeting thoughts were interrupted as Paul reached down and pushed her hand so that the knife cut through the cake.

"What're you dreaming about?" He laughed. "Everybody is waiting to taste the cake."

Lisa gave herself a mental shake and turned to the job at hand. She helped her mother cut and serve the cake and ice cream, and when everyone had eaten she went looking for Dave to ask him to turn on the stereo he had rigged up to loudspeakers over the garage.

"Not just yet, Lisa," he said when she found him in the kitchen. "We have a surprise for you first. Come on back outside and I'll make the announcement.''

Lisa had no idea what he was talking about but she followed him out and settled down on the lawn with the rest of the kids.

''We thought you might enjoy some special entertainment tonight,'' Dave began. ''So I've asked a friend of mine to join us.''

A man walked over from the side of the house where he had been standing unnoticed.

''I'd like you all to meet Merlin the Magician,'' Dave said in introduction. ''I think you're going to enjoy his performance.''

''Oh, no,'' Lisa groaned, burying her head on Paul's shoulder. ''How mortifying . . . a magician.'' She looked up and made a face at him. ''How could they do this to me?''

''What are you talking about?'' Paul looked down at her in surprise. ''Isn't he any good?''

''I don't know whether he's any good or not. But the kids don't want to see a magician. That's for children. They'd rather dance.''

Paul glanced around him. ''They all seem perfectly happy to me.''

Dave had set up a card table for Merlin to use and the magician was busy laying out his props. He began his act with some small sleight of hand tricks with coins and cards and scarves. It became obvious very quickly that he was a real professional and within minutes everyone was applauding madly as he finished each trick.

Lisa relaxed. She was enjoying the show as much as everyone else and before long she was ready to admit she had been wrong. Merlin was the perfect addition to make the evening a smashing success.

The backyard was lit now with floodlights from the house and garage. Eerie shapes and shadows from trees and bushes flickered in the background, lending a magical air to the sleight of hand deceptions being practiced by the adept magician. Although Lisa knew they were only tricks, the effects were stunning and the applause Merlin received echoed loudly through the night air.

After Merlin had packed up his props and gone on his way, wishing her a happy birthday, Lisa moved through the guests to her mother and Dave.

"Thank you," she said with sincere gratitude. "It was a wonderful surprise and everybody loved it."

Her mother slipped an arm through her husband's. "It was Dave's idea," she said quietly. "Merlin is a friend of Dave's and he made all the arrangements."

Lisa looked at Dave with a tentative smile. "It was very nice of you. Thank you again."

"I'm glad you enjoyed it." Dave's voice held no emotion and Lisa stood silently as he turned and led her mother into the house.

Paul came up behind her and grabbed her hand. "Come on, let's get in at least one dance before I have to leave."

"Leave?" His words brought her suddenly back to attention. "Where are you going? The party's just beginning."

"I told you I had a meeting tonight." He slipped his right arm around her waist and guided her around the driveway in time to the music pouring forth from the speakers. "They've called an organizational meeting for everyone who's going to work on the town's float for the Rose Parade." He looked at her quizzically. "I'm sure I told you about it."

Lisa did vaguely remember his mentioning something

when he had taken her to volunteer to do the makeup for the girls on the float. But she hadn't realized at the time that the meeting was tonight; in fact, she was sure Paul had only said it would be held during the Thanksgiving holidays.

"But I can't go to a meeting tonight," she began.

"You don't have to," Paul cut in. "You're not going to be helping with the decorating of the float, and now that the committee knows you'll be there to help the girls—"

"But I don't want you to go either," she blurted out. "It's my birthday, Paul. It's my party."

"Lisa," he said patiently, "I've been here over two hours already." He glanced at his watch over her shoulder. "And there's still half an hour before I have to leave. The meeting isn't until eight-thirty."

She pulled back from him slightly. "But I don't want you to go at all."

Paul looked regretful. "I know you don't and I don't really want to go either, but I have to. It's an obligation."

She pushed herself out of his arms and stood, fists clenched at her side. "Don't you think you have an obligation to me? You knew you were my date tonight, you knew how important my sixteenth birthday was to me."

"Lisa." Paul reached out to touch her shoulder, but she shrugged him off.

"I suppose you're taking Kayla to the meeting with you tonight?"

Paul looked bewildered. "What does Kayla have to do with this?"

"Is she going with you?" Lisa demanded, gesturing across the yard where Kayla stood talking with several friends.

Paul was getting angry. "As it happens, she is going with me. She's on the committee." He looked around him. "Brian and Rob and Margie are going too."

"Oh, that's just great." Lisa was furious now. "My party is going to break up because this town is having a stupid float in the Rose Parade."

"Lisa, there are thirty other kids here. Five of us are leaving. You'll never miss us." He grinned at her. "Well, on second thought, I hope you'll miss me."

But Lisa didn't want to be mollified by his teasing. She was furious that he was leaving and as he tried to gently tug her closer to his chest, she twisted out of his grip and stepped back. Several of the couples dancing near them looked at them curiously, and Lisa knew she had to control herself in front of her friends.

"I think you should leave now." She spoke through tight lips. "I wouldn't want you to be late for your meeting. Obviously, you'd rather be there than here."

She turned and walked away, leaving Paul standing on the driveway, a resigned look on his face. Holly and Floffy, talking quietly together near the back steps, greeted Lisa as she hurried by, intent on reaching her room before anyone could see the tears streaming down her cheeks.

"Wasn't Merlin terrific, Lisa?" Holly's excited voice reached Lisa through the hammering in her head.

Lisa half turned and gave her friend a tight smile through the shadowed light. "Yes, terrific."

Without saying more she hurried into the house, past a startled Potsy busy washing dishes at the sink, and into the bathroom. She quickly doused her face in cold water and tried to get a grip on her emotions. She ran a comb through her rumpled hair and applied a fresh coat of lip gloss. She was not going to ruin this evening by crying over Paul Webster.

As she went back outside, she saw Paul and Kayla and the other three walking up the driveway toward the front of the house. Holly stood off to the side watching. Suddenly, Lisa knew she couldn't let him leave like that. She ran after him, calling his name. Paul stopped and turned to look at her while the others went on ahead.

"I . . . I'm sorry, Paul. I didn't mean it," she stammered.

Paul sighed softly and shook his head. "I don't think you know what you mean half the time, Lisa." He leaned over and kissed her gently on the cheek, then followed the others out to the car.

The party went on until after midnight and the crowd seemed to be having a great time. Potsy served donuts and hot chocolate just before the guests were ready to go home, and when everyone but Holly and Floffy cleared out, Lisa's mother collapsed wearily on the living room sofa.

"Whew!" She let out a big sigh. "Lisa, I think we were a smashing success."

Her mother and Dave had stayed unobtrusively in the background most of the evening and Lisa had seen a number of her friends chatting with them off and on during the party. The word had gotten around that Lisa's stepfather was in the TV industry and a lot of the kids were impressed with that, wanting to know what stars he knew and what they were really like in person.

She had noticed that Dave always answered their questions graciously, never talking down to her friends or playing the role of big shot stage designer. For some reason that annoyed Lisa even more. She would have been happier if her friends hadn't liked him or if they had accused him of being a phony.

"It was a great party, all right." Holly kicked off her shoes and settled down on the living room rug, tucking her feet under her. Floffy sat behind her, legs outstretched so that she could lean back against him.

Lisa watched them covertly. They were so at ease and so right for each other. Their romance had gone smoothly from the day they had gotten together. Lisa thought of her own relationship with Paul. She was crazy about him, and she was pretty sure that he felt the same about her, yet they always seemed to be arguing about something. She had the nagging feeling that Paul disapproved of her somehow. She didn't want to think about why.

And him. He was always so damn perfect. Why did he always have to say and do exactly the right thing? Like tonight, for instance. He had an obligation to the float committee and he never thought twice about not meeting it, not even for a special occasion like her party.

Her mother suddenly gave a big yawn and Dave laughed at her affectionately. "Come on, little mother." He helped her up off the couch. "It's time you hit the sack."

Floffy and Holly stood up to say good night and Lisa kissed her mother and hugged her.

"Thanks, Mom," she whispered in her ear. "It was a terrific party."

Her mother pulled back a little to look at her. "I'm sorry it wasn't perfect for you, Lisa," she said softly.

Lisa lowered her eyes. She knew her mother had been aware of Paul's departure and now she wondered if her mother had also witnessed the big argument. She glanced up at Dave, but he was looking at her with the bland, uninvolved expression he had adopted the last few weeks, ever since their angry dispute on Halloween.

"Thank you for getting Merlin tonight," Lisa said again to him. "Everybody loved him. It really made the party."

For a moment a small smile warmed Dave's closed expression, then his face went blank once more as he nodded slightly. "I'm glad you were pleased, Lisa."

Lisa bit her lip in dismay. Dave's attitude toward her was making her very uncomfortable. She knew it was her own fault. This was the way she had wanted him to treat her. But now that he was doing it, somehow it was all wrong.

As her mother and Dave left the room, Holly gathered up her sweater and Floffy's jacket and started toward the front door.

"I've had it," she groaned. "My feet are killing me and I'm exhausted." She threw her arms around Lisa and gave her a hug. "Come over in the morning and we'll have a gab session about the party, okay?"

"Sure," Lisa agreed. "But not too early."

After she had locked the door behind them, she stuck her head in the kitchen, intending to say good night to Potsy and thank her again, but the housekeeper had already left for her own apartment. A feeling of depression settled over Lisa. The evening hadn't gone at all the way she had planned. Tomorrow, when she went over to the Websters', she would apologize properly to Paul and tell him she hadn't meant anything she said.

But the next morning, as she walked around the hedge and up the Webster driveway, she saw that Paul's car was gone and, although she and Holly sat in Holly's bedroom for hours chewing over every minute of the previous evening, Paul never came back. She accepted Mrs. Webster's invitation to stay for lunch, but even that was fruitless.

By three o'clock she couldn't drag out her visit any longer and, disconsolate, she wandered back to her own yard, crawling into her hide-a-way under the hedge. She stayed there for an hour, plucking at the leaves around her, trying to figure out why everything in her life seemed to be going wrong.

As usual on Saturday night, her mother and Dave were going out and Potsy left early. Lisa sat alone in her bedroom with the radio turned to a rock station, but barely heard the music. She knew Holly and Floffy were going to the movies, and when she glanced at the clock and saw that it was only seven-thirty, she wondered how she would get through this long, lonely night alone.

The picture of her father on her nightstand caught her eye and she picked it up, staring at it intently. The handsome face looked blankly back at her and Lisa suddenly realized how many lonely nights her mother had spent alone until Dave came into her life. "Why?" she whispered to the picture. "Why did you have to go and leave us alone?"

The sound of the doorbell startled her and she hurriedly put the picture back on the nightstand and went to see who was at the door. When she looked through the peephole and saw Paul standing on the front stoop, her heart began to beat wildly.

She fumbled with the deadbolt, conflicting thoughts racing through her mind. Had he come to tell her that he didn't want to see her anymore? Maybe he was going to say he couldn't drive her to school Monday morning. But that was silly. He wouldn't come over, especially on a

Saturday night, to say something like that.

She finally got the bolt drawn and yanked open the door. He stood there, hands in his pockets, a tentative smile on his lips.

"Hi." He looked beyond her into the house. "Are you alone?"

She nodded, afraid to trust her voice.

He walked past her into the den and flopped on the sofa. "Holly and Floffy are going to a movie. Do you want to go?"

"No." Her voice sounded rough and she cleared her throat. "No, thank you. I don't think I'm in the mood for sitting through a movie."

He nodded. "I feel the same way, but I thought you might want to do it."

She sat down opposite him and primly folded her hands. "How was your meeting last night?" she asked politely.

"Okay." He seemed uninterested in the subject.

"Did you have another meeting today?" She couldn't stop herself from asking. She was sure he had gone out today to avoid seeing her.

Paul shook his head. "I had to do something with my dad today. We were in Long Beach at my grandparents' house."

Lisa felt a tremendous sense of relief. Why hadn't she simply asked Holly where he was? It would have been so much simpler than worrying and fretting about it all day.

"Would you like something to eat?" She smiled at him, feeling a lot better now.

Paul laughed. "Well, I just finished dinner but I could always use a piece of one of Potsy's cakes."

"Good." She jumped up. "There's some of my birthday cake left. Would you like that?''

"Yeah, that was a terrific cake."

They went into the kitchen and she cut him a generous slice of the leftover cake and poured him a glass of milk. She took a smaller piece for herself and listened contenttedly as Paul explained between mouthfuls about the prefab storage shed he and his father had set up for his grandparents that afternoon.

After Lisa rinsed the dishes and glasses, they wandered back into the den. Paul settled back on the sofa once again, pulling her down beside him.

"I wasn't sure you'd want to see me tonight.'' He slipped his arm around her shoulders.

"Paul, I'm really sorry about last night," she began.

He placed a finger gently over her lips to stop her. "It wasn't all your fault. I should have made sure you understood I had to leave. In fact, I probably should have gotten out of the meeting. I knew how important your birthday party was to you.'' A small frown creased his forehead. "You're such a special girl, Lisa, and I know you're not very happy. I shouldn't have done anything to add to that unhappiness."

"Paul, that isn't true." She slipped her arms around him and leaned her head into the curve of his neck and shoulder. "I'm happy when I'm with you."

He rubbed his chin across her forehead before pulling back to look down into her eyes. "That isn't enough, Lisa. I wish I could get through to you about your feelings for your family, but I don't know how.'' He leaned forward and kissed her gently. "I want to make everything right for you."

"You do, Paul. When I'm with you, everything is perfect.'' She put her arms around his neck and kissed him back with growing fervor.

But his sympathetic words echoed through her mind and she knew he was right. She wondered if she would ever be completely happy again.

CHAPTER NINE

The three weeks between Thanksgiving and Christmas vacation passed swiftly in a blur of activity. At home, Lisa's mother was constantly on the phone or shopping or wrapping packages in her room. Potsy spent her days cooking and baking for the holidays, and the sweet smell of chocolate or orange or coconut constantly teased Lisa's nostrils. The house held an underlying sense of excitement Lisa couldn't remember ever experiencing before. Her mother was obviously pregnant now, and Lisa was aware of an air of expectancy that hovered over Sandra and Dave as the baby's arrival drew closer each day.

Lisa had long ago settled into the routine at school and she had to admit there were times when she felt as if she had never attended school anyplace else. Her work with the drama department filled her extra-curricular hours, and Dandy Andy had already asked her to supervise all the makeup for the big musical comedy the school put on annually in April. The students in the drama department had voted to do *The Music Man* this year; it had a huge cast and Lisa knew her work would be cut out for her when the time came.

On the last afternoon before school closed for Christmas vacation, Lisa hurried down the hall to the arts and crafts room. Jill Rollins, a friend of hers who was an excellent artist, had agreed to make the gift Lisa wanted to give Holly for Christmas. Lisa had taken a photo of Scruffy which Jill transferred onto a specially treated piece of leather. Then, by some method Lisa didn't really understand, Jill etched the picture into the leather so that it looked almost three-dimensional. When Lisa saw the finished piece she couldn't believe how beautiful it was.

"Thank you, Jill," she exclaimed. "You are so talented."

Jill laughed her thanks for the compliment as she wrapped the picture in a piece of brown paper before handing it to Lisa. "Not any more talented than you," she remarked. "In your own way, you're an artist too. I thought the makeup you did for *Death of a Salesman* was fantastic. The kids really looked as if they were our parents' age instead of ours."

Now it was Lisa's turn to murmur her thanks. "Are you going to study art professionally?" she asked her friend.

Jill nodded. "I'm going to study at the art center in Pasadena after I graduate. Where are you planning to go?"

Lisa had been thinking about college for some time now, although she didn't have to make a definite decision for over a year. Paul had already been accepted at UCLA for the following September, to study pre-med. Lisa knew UCLA had an outstanding theater arts department and with her grades she shouldn't have any problem at all being accepted on the Westwood campus. But her mother had often expressed the opinion that it was a good idea for teenagers to go away from home, at least for their first two years of higher education. And with her home situation the way it was now—Lisa's antagonism toward Dave and the new baby coming—she was sure her mother would be more convinced than ever that Lisa should look outside of Los Angeles to choose her university.

"I'm not sure yet," Lisa told Jill. "Someplace that has a good theater department. Someone was telling me about the University of Arizona."

"Yes, I heard it's an excellent school for theater," Jill agreed. "I have a cousin who went there to study design."

Lisa picked up Holly's present and moved toward the door. "Thanks again, Jill. I know Holly's going to love it. Remember now"—she raised a warning finger—"don't say anything if you see her before the holidays."

Jill laughed. "Don't worry, I won't spoil your surprise. Merry Christmas," she added gaily, "if I don't see you again."

Lisa turned in the doorway. "Aren't you going to the Christmas dance tonight?"

Jill shook her head. "I'm going up to the mountains with my parents for the holidays. We like to spend them up in the snow. I'll see you when I get back."

Lisa thanked her again and hurried out to the front of the school where Paul was waiting to drive her home.

"What's that?" he asked pointing to the bulky package.

"A Christmas present," she said nonchalantly.

He raised an eyebrow. "Someone gave you a Christmas present already?"

"No, it's something I bought for someone else."

"For me," he said gleefully. He reached out and

grabbed the edge of the package. "You're giving me a piece of wood for Christmas?"

"Stop that." She snatched it out of his grasp, laughing. "It isn't a piece of wood and it isn't for you."

"Is it for your mother?" he asked, looking over at her as he stopped for a red light.

"No." She shook her head.

"For Dave then?" he said, "or Potsy?"

"Nope."

Paul's smile faded. "Another guy?" he asked quietly.

A horn behind them honked as the light turned green. Paul shifted the gears and drove slowly on.

"Don't be silly," Lisa said gently. "You know there isn't any other guy I'd give a present to. It's for Holly, but if you say anything to her, I'll kill you." She looked at him with a threatening frown.

Paul relaxed against the seat back, "I won't say anything. Boy, she's going to be thrilled, getting a piece of wood for Christmas."

"I told you—it isn't a piece of wood," Lisa began, then realized he was baiting her, trying to get her to tell him what was in the package. "Let's talk about something else," she said primly. "As far as this package is concerned, my lips are sealed."

Paul turned into the driveway of his house and switched off the ignition. "I know how to unseal them," he said softly. He leaned over and kissed her, proceeding to do just that. "I'll pick you up at eight o'clock," he murmured as she started to get out of the car, and Lisa nodded in agreement.

She hurried around the hedge and across the lawn, clutching her books and Holly's package tightly in her hands. She was planning on a long leisurely soak in a

bubble bath before she did her nails and hair for the big
Christmas dance that night. And after she had greeted
Potsy and her mother she hurried to her room to begin
getting ready.

The bubble bath relaxed her and made her slightly
sleepy, so that her mind wandered aimlessly from subject
to subject. At one point she drew up a mental list of all the
things Paul might be giving her for Christmas, running all
the way from a bottle of perfume to his class ring. But after
indulging her fantasies for endless moments she decided
that his mother would probably advise him to choose
something more sensible, like handkerchiefs or a book, or
maybe a new record for her stereo.

By the time she had finished her nails and set her hair, it
was time for dinner. Lisa's mother smilingly gave her
daughter permission to have a quick bite in the kitchen
before returning to her room to begin the delicate makeup
application. In spite of her expertise in the field, Lisa
rarely used anything besides lipstick and a bit of mascara
during the week. On date nights she added a touch of
blusher and an occasional swipe of eyeshadow. But tonight's dance was the biggest event of the social year at
school and Lisa wanted to look her absolute best. She
started out with a light film of base followed by a pink
blusher across her high cheekbones. She filled in her
eyebrow line with a light feathering, then added a faint
shadow of white under the arch of the brow. A dusty
mauve eyeshadow came next, then a line of black eyeliner
directly over her lashes. Above that she applied a faint
streak of silver. After curling her lashes and applying
mascara, she drew a faint line under her eye with a mauve
pencil. As a last touch she outlined her lips with a pink
liner slightly darker than the color of the lipstick she

planned to use. A finishing touch of gloss created exactly the look she wanted. When she was finished she removed the makeup band she had placed around her face and brushed out her hair.

She had just pulled her gown out of the closet when there was a light tap on the door.

"Lisa, may I come in?"

It was her mother's voice, and Lisa called out to her to come in.

"Here, let me help you," she said, reaching for the dress.

It was an ankle-length gown in a deep shade of pink that Lisa had bought last spring for a dance at her old school. She loved the dress, and since no one in this school had ever seen it, she and her mother had agreed there was no point in buying something new. Her mother zipped up the back for her and fluffed up the puffy sleeves. Lisa pirouetted in front of her.

"What do you think?"

"You look beautiful." Her mother's hands were clasped over her swelling abdomen. She frowned slightly. "Your makeup looks beautiful, honey, but don't you think perhaps you have a bit too much on?"

"Oh, Mom, don't be silly," Lisa protested. "You know I don't do this very often." She turned to examine herself in the full-length mirror on the door. "I just wanted to look special tonight."

Her mother came up behind her and slipped an arm around her shoulders. "You are special, Lisa," she said softly.

Lisa could see the sadness in her mother's eyes as she watched her in the mirror.

"I'm sorry this has been such an unhappy time for you.

Sometimes I . . . I feel as if it's all my fault . . . maybe I shouldn't have . . .''

Lisa turned swiftly and put her arms around her mother. ''Don't be silly, Mom. You know that half the time I don't mean what I say. Of course you did the right thing.''

Her mother gave a wry smile and slipped out of her embrace. ''You'd better finish getting dressed, honey. Paul will be here in a few minutes.'' She turned and left the room.

Lisa knew her mother didn't believe what she had said. But she couldn't stand that sad look in her eyes, and things had been a lot better lately. Ever since Dave had decided it was fruitless to try and make friends with her, the harsh words and angry scenes had stopped. Their relationship certainly wasn't a normal one, but at least it had stopped being an antagonistic one. Lisa knew that her mother had hoped for more than that. But Lisa also knew it wasn't ever going to be.

The look on Paul's face when he walked in and saw her was compliment enough, but she felt an added thrill when he said, ''Gosh, you look fantastic!''

''Thank you,'' she murmured, feeling suddenly shy.

He peered at her closely. ''It isn't just the dress. You look . . . I don't know . . . different.''

''Different, how?'' Lisa asked innocently, knowing it was the makeup that had made the change.

Paul shrugged. ''I don't know. Older, I guess.''

''Too old?'' She began to wonder if maybe her mother was right.

An affectionate smile appeared on his lips. ''Nope, just perfect. Come on.'' He held her coat open so she could slip her arms into it easily. ''Holly and Floffy are waiting for us in the car.''

117

After saying good night to her mother and Dave, they went out to meet the other couple in Floffy's car.

When they got to the school gymnasium where the dance was being held, Holly motioned for Lisa to follow her into the girl's room.

"I couldn't wait to tell you," Holly said, obviously excited about something. "Look at what Floffy gave me." She pointed to a beautiful gold heart-shaped locket hanging on a delicate chain around her neck. "He couldn't wait until Christmas to give it to me." A delighted smile wreathed her sunny face. "And look what's inside." She snapped open the locket to reveal a tiny picture of Floffy himself on one side and some funny-looking black stuff on the other.

"What's that?" Lisa pointed to it.

"A lock of his hair, silly," Holly said. "What did you think it was?"

"Oh, Holly," Lisa sighed. "That really is romantic."

"I know," Holly agreed. "It's practically Victorian." She hunched her shoulders with glee. "I've never been so excited in my life."

"What did your mom and day say?" Lisa wondered. "I mean, that's a pretty personal present."

"It's not personal," Holly said defensively. "It's . . . it's special."

"Did they say it was okay for you to take it?" Lisa knew Holly well enough by now to know that it wouldn't be like her to go against her parents' wishes.

"My mom said it was a lovely gift, my dad didn't say much of anything, and Paul"—she paused for a moment, a puzzled look on her face—"Paul looked kind of surprised."

Lisa felt her heart sink. Did that mean Paul was surprised by the gift itself or did it mean that he was surprised Floffy had given Holly a Christmas present at all? Maybe he had never thought about giving Lisa a gift. Maybe when Christmas morning came and it was time to hand him the very special book she had chosen with her mother's help, one written by a young doctor about practicing modern medicine, there would be no gift in return for her.

She started to ask Holly if she knew what Paul had bought for her, but then she changed her mind. It wasn't fair to impose on her best friend that way simply because she was Paul's sister.

Some of their friends came into the girl's room as they stood talking.

"Floffy and Paul are looking for you two," one of them said. "They're starting to look restless!"

Holly and Lisa laughed and went back out to the gymnasium floor. The next few hours were marvelous. The live band played everything from country and western to old sentimental ballads to rock 'n' roll, even throwing in a few passé disco tunes. By the time they swung into the traditional "Good Night Ladies," Lisa's hair felt limp and her feet were sore, but her spirits were higher than they had been in months. She had had a thoroughly enjoyable evening.

On the way home much of the talk centered around the upcoming Rose Parade. As soon as Christmas was behind them the real work on the floats began, and she knew Paul would be tied up day and night until New Year's Day. She was looking forward to her own part in the float's preparation, although she wouldn't actually be involved until the last morning.

Floffy stopped the car in front of Lisa's house, and the

four sat talking quietly for another few minutes. Then Paul opened his door and came around to help Lisa out of the car, and Floffy drove into the Websters' driveway to escort Holly to her door.

Lisa and Paul strolled slowly arm in arm across her front lawn. The front porch light was on and Paul tugged her into the shadows beside the steps where he took her in his arms for a good night kiss. His lips felt warm and soft on hers and she delighted in the closeness of the embrace. They lingered in the darkness for endless moments until Paul finally led her up the steps and saw her into the house.

To her surprise, a light was still on in the den. Peering in, she found her mother and Dave, dressed in pajamas and robes, seated before a roaring fire, sipping eggnog, presenting a picture of total happiness and contentment.

"Lisa, honey, come and join us," her mother greeted her.

"What are you doing up so late?" Lisa wanted to know. "I thought the doctor said you had to get your rest."

"I am resting," her mother protested. "And besides, I had a long nap this afternoon." She smiled at her husband. "Dave and I decided it was time to get into the holiday spirit. After all, you had the dance tonight and I've been busy shopping . . ."

"I'll say," Lisa interrupted with a laugh. She settled into a chair near the sofa. "I saw all that stuff you dragged in from the car when you thought no one was looking."

Her mother shook a finger at her joshingly. "You always did turn into a little sneak at Christmas, Lisa. I thought you had outgrown spying on Santa Claus."

The three of them burst out laughing, and as Lisa pulled off her shoes and tucked her feet up on the chair under her gown, Dave stood up to hand her a mug of eggnog.

"Ummm, this is delicious." Lisa licked the froth of egg white and nutmeg from her upper lip. "Where did you get it?"

"Dave made it," her mother said. "Isn't it good?"

"Fantastic." Lisa took another big swallow. "Where did you learn to make this?" She looked over at Dave with a smile.

The expression on his face startled her. His eyes were wary, as if he expected her to turn into a screaming shrew at any minute. Lisa felt her smile fade. Dave thought she was putting on an act, lulling them into a mood of camaraderie so she could shatter it with one of her resentful tantrums.

It isn't true, she wanted to shout at him. I'm really enjoying myself. I like sitting here late at night in the quiet with you and my mother. I wish it could always be this way. I don't want you to look at me like that.

But she knew she couldn't say those things out loud, because if she did, she would be doing exactly what he expected of her. She gripped the mug tightly in her fingers and sat quietly for a few minutes more. But her mellow mood had disappeared. Once again she was feeling anger and guilt. She stood up, putting the mug down on the coffee table in front of them.

"Don't stay up too late now," she warned her mother gently as she leaned over to kiss her good night. "Remember what the doctor said." She nodded curtly in Dave's direction and left the room As she went out into the hall she heard the loud sigh her mother gave and Dave's voice murmur softly in response.

In her room she removed the pink dress and hung it up carefully in her closet. It had been a good day and a wonderful evening, up until the last few minutes. She pulled on her pajamas and sat down on the side of the bed, taking the picture of her father in her hands. All her life, his face had been familiar to her, sitting there by the side of her bed. But these last few months the realization had slowly dawned on her that if he were alive today, he probably· wouldn't look anything like the handsome young man in the picture. He had been caught in a moment of time by a photographer. He would always remain young and smiling and carefree. But the world in which he had lived no longer existed. The wife and daughter he had left behind had gone on to a new life and a different world.

She replaced the picture gently in its usual spot. For a long time she hadn't been able to understand how her mother could have replaced her father with another man. But lately a thought had come to her, unbidden: this wasn't her father. This was only a photograph, a piece of paper. It wasn't that her mother had replaced him with another man; it was simply that after too many years alone, her mother had moved ahead with her life.

CHAPTER TEN

Christmas morning dawned clear and cold. When Lisa woke up at six A.M. she told herself it was silly to get up this early at her age. Only little kids were so excited about opening their presents that they couldn't sleep. But what the hell, she was already awake, so she might as well get out of bed and go take a peek into the den. Dave had set up the Christmas tree there the night before, and watched while Lisa and her mother trimmed it with their favorite ornaments.

After so many years of doing it together, they knew just where they wanted each bell and snowflake to hang. Before long the tree had taken on that special look only a Christmas tree can have.

The house was still and quiet as Lisa crept down the hall, but there was an air of expectancy, almost as if the house knew that this day was different, that something exciting was about to happen.

In the den, Lisa bent down to plug in the lights of the tree, then she sat back, legs crossed in front of her, to admire the picture it made, green and fresh and glowing, gaily wrapped presents piled in front of it. After admiring the setting for a few minutes, she tiptoed into the kitchen to start the water boiling so there would be tea or coffee for Sandra and Dave to sip as they opened their gifts. She pulled a tray out of an overhead cupboard and put three cups and saucers, the sugar and creamer, and several holiday paper napkins on it.

She had just set the tray down on the coffee table in the den when her mother and Dave walked into the room, sleepy-eyed but smiling. Her mother wore a pale pink, loosely flowing dressing gown and Lisa thought she had never seen her look so pretty.

"Merry Christmas," she cried.

"Merry Christmas, darling," her mother replied, giving her a quick kiss.

"Merry Christmas, Lisa." Dave's voice came quietly from behind them.

Lisa turned and smiled tentatively. "Merry Christmas, Dave."

She could almost feel the tension leave her mother's body. The sensation shook Lisa to the core. *She was afraid of what I might say,* Lisa realized with sudden shock.

And then came further enlightenment. Her mother must live with this tension constantly, never knowing what Lisa would say next to Dave, never knowing when some little thing that he said or did would throw her into another childish tantrum. Lisa knew that kind of tension was the worst thing for her mother, especially since she was pregnant.

I'll be on my best behavior today, Lisa swore to herself. *Even if I have to bite my tongue till it falls off.*

No matter what her feelings were about Dave Hubbard, the last thing she wanted was to do anything to make her mother ill. The sound of the tea kettle whistling on the kitchen stove distracted her.

"What'll it be?" she asked cheerily. "Tea or coffee?"

A pleased look came over her mother's face at Lisa's thoughtfulness. "A pot of tea, I think, don't you, Dave?"

He nodded his agreement and Lisa dashed to the kitchen to fix it.

When she had returned with the steaming brew, they each took a cup and settled down to the serious business of opening their gifts. Lisa was in charge of parceling them out and she took the job seriously, giving each one enough time to open and savor each individual gift as it was presented to them.

There were the usual practical ones: pajamas and a shirt for Dave, a nightgown and pantyhose for her mother, and a new school purse and knee socks for Lisa. There were books and stationery and a subscription to a baby magazine for her mother that made them all laugh.

Then it was time for the special gifts, the ones that had taken the most thought and imagination. Dave gave Sandra a beautiful gold bracelet with earrings to match. Her gift to him was a slim, modern pen and pencil set. Lisa's present from her mother was a matching skirt and sweater set, one she had seen in a store on the avenue and had come home exclaiming about, never dreaming that her mother would remember and make the special effort to surprise her with it for the holiday.

The last unopened gift under the tree was for Lisa from Dave. It looked like a wooden box of some sort, and as she opened it her mind busily scurried, trying to figure out in advance what it could be. When she finally had the paper off and opened the lid she gasped with surprise. It was a professional makeup box, one that Dave had gotten from the studio. Without thinking, Lisa jumped up and ran to give him a huge hug of thanks, forgetting for a moment who had given her this magnificent gift. But as soon as she touched him she realized what she was doing and, with an embarrassed laugh, she backed away and stood speechless, staring at him. Finally, swallowing hard, she managed to get out the words.

"Thank you, Dave, it's fabulous." She felt herself flushing. "It was very nice of you to think of it." She knew her words sounded stilted but the situation had gotten out of control. Her instinctive reaction to the gift had gone against all of her previous behavior. She could see by the look on Dave's face that it had embarrassed him as much as it had her.

Her mother came to the rescue. "Now I know why you wouldn't tell me what it was." A happy smile lit her face. "He refused to say one word, Lisa. I've been nagging and teasing him for weeks to tell me what was in there, but he absolutely refused."

Dave laughed. "I didn't trust you. I know how you women are when it comes to keeping a secret."

"Oh!"

"How dare you!"

Lisa and her mother both reacted to the sexist remark.

But even though they were all laughing hilariously, a little part of Lisa stood back detached, knowing that underneath all the joking there was a serious thread in what Dave had said. Lisa knew why Dave hadn't told her mother about the special gift. He had feared that her mother might use the knowledge to bribe Lisa into changing her mind about him. Lisa was constantly aware of the pleading look in her mother's eyes when the three of them were together. It was one reason Lisa had tried so hard not to be around the two of them, except at meals.

Abruptly Lisa turned away, picking up her mother's new housecoat and holding it out to her.

"Come on, Mom," she said. "Try it on and let's see how it fits."

"Oh, dear," her mother said ruefully. "I'm getting so big, I don't think anything is going to fit."

"Nonsense." Dave was emphatic. "You look wonderful. Lisa's right, try it on and let's see how it looks."

"All right." Her mother left the room with the new robe over her arm.

While she was gone, Dave and Lisa proceeded to clean up some of the mess of crumpled papers and torn ribbons littered around the floor. Her mother returned in a few minutes and Lisa and Dave exclaimed at how attractive she looked in her new robe.

"Here, Mom, you forgot one of the buttons." Lisa reached out and started to pull the button through the buttonhole. Just as she did, she felt a sharp bump against her hand. Startled, she looked at her mother. "What was that?"

"That was the baby kicking," her mother said, grinning.

"You're kidding!"

Her mother took Lisa's hand and held it flat against her stomach. "Here, maybe you can feel it again."

"When did that start?" She looked quickly from Dave to her mother.

"It's been weeks," her mother said.

"Why didn't you ever let me feel it before?"

"I didn't think you were interested." Her mother's

voice was quiet. "Everything about this baby seems to upset you."

Lisa felt tears forming in her eyes. "Mom, that isn't true. It isn't the baby, it's . . ."

"Lisa, please." Her mother looked away. "Let's not spoil today."

"I won't, Mom, I promise," she muttered. "I don't want you to get upset."

Dave sighed and went back to the mess under the Christmas tree. "Come on, Lisa." His voice had returned to that neutral tone he always used with her. "Let's get this cleaned up and get dressed."

The sound of the back door slamming relieved the tension in the room somewhat. Potsy had arrived, and her presence always acted as a buffer to the conflicting currents between the three of them.

"Good morning," she cried cheerily as she walked into the den, her arms filled with packages. "And a Happy Yuletide to all of you."

Once she had distributed her gifts to them and they had reciprocated, she set off for the kitchen to make what she called a special Christmas breakfast.

It turned out to be not only special, but enormous. When they were through, the three of them swore that they wouldn't be able to eat one bite of the Christmas dinner that was planned for two o'clock.

"You'll eat," Potsy predicted. "I'm not worried about any of your appetites. And besides, if you're not hungry it'll just mean more for the company."

They were expecting a houseful of people to join them. Lisa and her mother had no family in California, but Dave had a sister and brother-in-law with two small children, and a number of friends had also been invited.

Lisa took her gifts to her room and changed into a pair of jeans and a velour shirt.

At ten o'clock the front door bell rang. Lisa ran to open it, and Paul and Holly stood there, broad grins on their faces and gifts in their hands.

"Come in," Lisa cried. "Merry Christmas."

"Merry Christmas," they chorused.

Dave and her mother came to see who was at the door, and in a few minutes they were all back in the den, once again opening gifts. Lisa loved the pair of earrings that Holly had selected for her and she was thrilled when she saw how excited Holly was with her leather picture of Scruffy.

"How fantastic!" Holly exclaimed. "How did you ever think of it, Lisa?"

"I saw another one that Jill had done," Lisa admitted. "I knew it was the right thing as soon as I saw it."

Holly hugged it to her. "But now you'll have to get me another one," she said, a sparkle of excitement in her eyes.

"What are you talking about?"

"You haven't seen my Christmas present from Paul yet," Holly went on. "He got me a new puppy!"

Lisa gave a surprised laugh. "You got another dog? But . . . but . . . what about Scruffy?"

"What about him?" Holly looked as if she didn't understand.

"Well, Scruffy is your dog. Isn't he going to be awfully hurt if there's a new puppy in the house?"

"Don't be silly." Holly waved her comment aside. "Come on, open Paul's present. I can't wait to see your face."

Paul's gift was an oddly shaped, knobby-looking, large

package, almost as tall as her waist. Lisa ran tentative fingers over the outside trying to guess what was in it. But everyone yelled at her to stop cheating.

Eagerly she ripped the paper off and stood in happy amazement. It was a makeup table, a boxlike arrangement set on sturdy legs, complete with hinged mirror. Lisa had seen similar ones when the professional makeup artists had let her watch them on the set of the TV show.

"Oh, Paul," she breathed. "This is fantastic." She squeezed his hand. "How did you ever think of it?"

"I have to admit the original idea was Dave's," he said. "He knew that the arrangement you have in your room isn't very good and when he told me about the makeup box he was getting you—"

"You knew about that?" Lisa interrupted.

"Fine thing," her mother added, pretending to be hurt. "He wouldn't say a word to me."

Paul laughed. "He had to tell me because I had to know what size to make the table."

Lisa realized that Paul had made the table himself. She ran a hand gently over the polished wood. That made it even more special, knowing it must have taken him hours of painstaking work.

After Paul had opened his gift and exclaimed over the book, Lisa took Holly to her room to show her all the gifts she had received earlier. Holly recited the litany of her own "haul" and finished by saying, "You'll see Peanuts tonight when you come over."

Lisa and the Hubbards had been invited to the Websters' for a light Christmas-night snack after all the family company had gone home. Mrs. Webster called it "the unwinding," a chance to ease back into the normal routine after all the excitement of the holiday. Holly had told Lisa that they did it every year, usually with just one other family. "It keeps you from feeling that post-holiday let-down," she had explained. "We'll have fun."

After Paul and Holly left, Lisa showered and dressed in preparation for the sumptuous Christmas dinner Potsy had slaved over for a week. By one o'clock the house was filled with laughing, chatting people, and promptly at two o'clock, they sat down to an enormous dinner that started with fresh fruit cup and ended with mince pie and plum pudding for dessert.

Lisa enjoyed having a house full of guests, but several times during the afternoon she found herself thinking ahead to the evening at the Websters', wondering how it would be with the two families alone, something that had not happened since the Hubbards had moved in that summer.

When the last of their dinner guests had finally departed, Dave insisted that her mother lie down and rest for a while before they ventured next door. It was after seven o'clock when they finally walked into the Websters' living room. Dr. Webster had a roaring fire going in the fireplace and Mrs. Webster offered a tray with champagne for the adults and a variety of soft drinks for Lisa, Holly, and Paul.

"Come and meet Peanuts," Holly said as soon as they had removed their coats. She grabbed Lisa's hand and dragged her into the kitchen.

A small dog basket had been placed in the breakfast area and in it lay a tiny, golden bundle of fur. Holly picked the puppy up and handed it to Lisa.

"Maybe you'll like her better than you do Scruffy since she's only a baby."

"Why does everybody think I don't like Scruffy?" Lisa

protested, as the ball of fur snuggled in her arms.

"You were pretty definite about it when you first moved here," Holly said. "You know you hated him. Well, didn't you?"

"It did take me a while to get used to him," Lisa admitted reluctantly. "I'd never been around dogs much before. But he doesn't bother me anymore. In fact, I really like him."

"I love him," Holly said simply.

She took the puppy from Lisa's arms and put her back in the basket.

"That's what I don't understand," Lisa said. "I know you love Scruffy, so how can you get another dog? Now they're going to have to share your love."

Holly looked at Lisa as if she thought she was crazy. "You make it sound as if I only have so much love and I'm going to have to chop it up in little pieces and spread it around. I don't love Scruffy any less because Peanuts has arrived. My loving Scruffy has nothing to do with my loving Peanuts."

A noise in the doorway made Lisa look up. Paul was standing there, his arms folded, a strange look on his face. Lisa knew immediately what he was thinking. He was drawing a parallel between Holly's relationship with the dog, and Lisa and the new baby.

But they're not the same, she thought wildly. It's not the same thing at all.

"No," she said out loud before she could stop herself.

Paul didn't answer. He just shook his head slowly and turned away.

Holly looked perplexed. "What was that all about?"

Lisa didn't answer her. She went back to the den and sat quietly beside her mother.

Dave and Dr. Webster were having an animated discussion about football while her mother and Mrs. Webster talked about Sandra's pregnancy. Paul and Holly settled themselves in front of the fire. Holly worked on a small needlepoint picture while Paul stretched out and stared intently into the glowing embers.

Mrs. Webster had just started serving sandwiches when Floffy wandered in to join them. Once again Lisa was taken with how easily he fit in to the Websters' family circle and how smoothly his relationship had developed with Holly.

Before long the conversation turned to the subject of the Rose Parade and the town float. Work would begin in earnest the following week on the final stages, and Paul explained to the rest of them exactly how some of the decorative foliage was attached to the frames of the spectacular displays.

Mrs. Webster brought out a huge fruitcake and served coffee and tea along with it. By nine o'clock everyone was exhausted from the long exciting day, and Dave insisted it was time for Lisa's mother to get to bed.

Holly and Floffy wanted to take a short walk before calling it a night and Lisa and Paul decided to join them. They strolled down the block through the crisp, cold air, returning finally to say good night at Lisa's driveway. As the other two went on toward Holly's house, Paul walked Lisa to the door, giving her a warm kiss good night.

"Thank you again for my table, Paul," she whispered. "It was a wonderful present."

"So was yours." He leaned over and rubbed his cold nose against hers.

He looked at her intently for a long moment. "I heard what Holly was saying to you in the kitchen, Lisa."

Instinctively she backed away.

"Don't get sore." He tugged her back against him. "I'm not going to give you another lecture, but just think about what she said. It was true, every word of it."

He brushed her lips with his once more, then opened the door and pushed her inside. "Merry Christmas," he murmured and walked away.

Lisa closed the door and locked it and walked slowly to her room. It *had* been a merry Christmas, one of the best and happiest she could ever remember. Last year at this time she and her mother had still been alone, and even though they had celebrated with friends, it had been nothing like the joyful, noisy holiday of this year.

She cleared her presents off the bed and stacked them on a chair. Paul's table sat by the window with Dave's gift on top of it. They were two of the most thoughtful and special gifts she had ever received, and Paul had said that both of them were Dave's idea.

With a shrug, Lisa turned away and took her nightgown out of the closet. She didn't want to think about that tonight; it might ruin the whole day if she did. But she was aware that the time was rapidly approaching when she would have to settle the confusion in her mind once and for all.

CHAPTER ELEVEN

Lisa hardly saw Paul for the next few days. It was almost like last summer when he had been working for his uncle's construction company: he left the house early in the morning and worked later and later each night as New Year's Day drew closer.

Two days before the parade, Lisa went to the high school and did a dry run on the makeup for the girls on the float. The local committee had also asked her to help with the costumes, and they spent the entire day pinning and tucking and shortening and draping. Because the costumes were authentically Japanese, several women from the Japanese community had been asked to come in and help. It took several hours to put on the costumes correctly and a number of dress rehearsals were needed before New Year's morning.

The warehouses where the floats were decorated were off-limits to everyone except the crews who did the actual decorating. People riding on the floats, however, were permitted to come in to see how the work was progressing and were even invited to help with the gigantic task.

When the three princesses who were to ride on their local float decided to go up and see the work in progress, Lisa went along with them. She knew it would be one of the few opportunities she would have to see Paul—even for a few minutes—until after the parade.

It took Lisa and the girls a few minutes to locate their float. Most of the floats looked like weirdly shaped prehistoric monsters, with arcs and curves and half-circles of framework sticking up in the air. It was possible to put most of the greenery and wood on the float at this stage, but the flowers couldn't be added until the last possible moment, even though they were sprayed with a preservative, so that they would look fresh and bright the morning of the parade. The bulk of the fresh flowers would be added the day and evening before the parade, workers staying up most of the night to complete the enormous task.

"Hey, Lisa." Paul waved to her from the far side of the float where he was busy twining ivy around a wooden pole. "What are you doing here?"

Lisa explained that she had been to the dress rehearsal. "We decided to come over here and see how you guys were getting along."

Most of the daytime crews were school kids and women, each group consisting of four or five people. At night men from the community did their hitch, although some of them did take off from work for several days before the parade to help with the decorating.

"How about giving us a hand?" Paul said. "We can always use another worker."

"Sure, I'd love to," Lisa said. "Just let me call my

mom and tell her I'll be late.''

When that task had been accomplished, Lisa hurried back to pitch in, working under Paul's direction. He showed her how to twist and combine the vines and leaves, attaching them to the float frame with adhesives so they wouldn't fall off during the long ride down the parade route.

The pungent smell of damp leaves and ferns reminded Lisa of hiking through the woods when she had gone to camp in northern California. As the float took shape under their hands, Lisa began to appreciate the enormous amount of work and effort that went into the event.

By late afternoon her arms were aching and her fingers felt as if they had been rubbed raw, but the worst part of it was that she hardly saw Paul at all.

Holly had come in about an hour after Lisa to do her regular stint, and after putting the two girls to work at one end of the float, Paul seemed to have disappeared, although Lisa knew he was probably somewhere up on top, working on the Japanese style bridge. She caught a glimpse of him from time to time when he hopped down to get more material or to take a hasty look at the job they were doing. But other than giving her a quick smile, he hardly seemed aware that she was even in the same room.

By five o'clock her shoulders were aching, her hands hurt and her disposition was turning sour. She squatted back on her heels, looking at Holly who was still busy pasting orange buds around a post.

"I've had it," Lisa declared. "I'm exhausted. Come on, Holly, let's get going. It's quitting time."

Holly glanced at her watch. "I think I'll work for another hour. Floffy isn't coming until eight o'clock. That'll give me plenty of time to get home and change.

They need all the help they can get—there's only one more full day before the parade.''

Lisa groaned as she stood up, every bone aching. "Paul hasn't said where we're going tonight. But I guess since it's Saturday night, we'll probably take in a flick.''

Holly looked at her strangely. "I didn't know you and Paul had a date tonight.''

"Well, actually he didn't ask me, but . . ." She stopped short. "Well, it is Saturday night and usually on Saturday night . . .''

"Lisa, I think you'd better check with him before you make any plans,'' Holly interrupted. "This is the second year that Paul has helped with the float and I know these last two nights he usually stays right on the job.'' She gestured upward. "You can see how much is left to do. They've only just started with the flowers. There are hours and hours more work.''

"I'm sure there must be another crew coming on tonight,'' Lisa said. "Everything else around here is well organized. They must have that planned too.''

"Sure they do,'' Holly agreed. "But these last two days they ask everyone to give all the time they can.''

"He's given enough time,'' Lisa argued. "I've hardly seen him all week, and the last couple of days . . .''

Holly turned and went back to work. "I think I'd better stay out of this,'' she said. "It's between you and Paul.''

Lisa knew how Paul felt about this obligation, but she had been sure they would do something tonight. Vacation was almost over. School started again Tuesday morning and it would be back to the regular routine.

She went looking for Paul and found him with several other boys, carting over a huge load of cut flowers.

"It's five o'clock, Paul,'' she said. "How much longer

are you going to stay here?''

Paul looked perplexed, as if he didn't understand her question. Then his expression cleared and he smiled. ''Are you getting hungry? We can break and go for a hamburger any time you like.''

''A hamburger? You mean before we go to a movie?''

Paul frowned. ''What movie? I'm not going to any movie. I'll probably be here till the early hours of the morning.''

''But I thought we had a date, Paul. It's Saturday night.''

Paul's face seemed to close up like a tight fist. ''So it's Saturday night. I told you weeks ago that I wouldn't be able to do anything these last few days. I thought you understood. But you never understand anything if it isn't what you want, do you, Lisa?'' He started to turn away.

''Paul, please.'' She reached out to grab his arm. ''I didn't mean . . .''

He shook her off. ''You never mean anything. Sometimes I wonder if you know yourself what you mean.''

''Paul.'' Her eyes filled with tears. ''Why are you talking to me like this?''

He gave a big sigh and walked back to her, slinging an arm around her shoulders. ''I'm sorry, I shouldn't have said that. Come on, let's get Holly and we'll go and get something to eat. We'll all feel better.''

''Holly's leaving,'' she said softly. ''She and Floffy have a date tonight.''

''Floffy doesn't work on the float,'' he said, watching her closely.

Lisa nodded. ''I know. I understand.''

''Let's get cleaned up and go get that hamburger,'' Paul

said. "You want to call your mother again?"

"I guess I'd better. I told her I'd be home for dinner and she'll be wondering where I am."

After Lisa had made her call and they had cleaned up in the washrooms, they climbed into the P1800 and drove to the Hamburger Shack, where they had gone that first time with Holly.

"How about it?" Paul asked with a grin as they sat at one of the small wooden tables. "Are you up to a dragon-burger?"

Lisa groaned. "I don't know. I'm so tired I don't know if my stomach will take it."

"Sure it will," Paul urged. "The chili will wake you up in a hurry."

After the waitress had taken their orders, they both sat back and tried to relax.

"It is a lot of hard work, isn't it, Paul? I hadn't realized."

"Most people don't," Paul said. "They see the beautiful floats rolling down the avenue on New Year's morning, with all the pretty girls standing there waving at the crowds, and they never stop to think of the hundreds of hours of work that went into making the floats look the way they do."

"Who comes up with the ideas for the floats?" Lisa asked.

"As soon as the parade is over, the committee gets busy right away, deciding on the overall theme for the next year," Paul explained. "Then each city or business or organization that's going to enter, decides on its own personal theme. Most of them contact a professional float builder who does the basic construction, although some of the entrants, like the Cal-Poly University campuses, build their own right from scratch. They make it an engineering project at the school and the kids see it through from the very beginning until the last flower goes on.''

Lisa shook her head in wonderment. "It really is an enormous undertaking. I never had any idea when I used to watch the parade on TV."

"Haven't you ever seen it in person?" Paul wondered.

"Years ago, when I was a little kid," Lisa said. "Some relatives of my mom's were here from New York and they wanted to see it. All I can remember is the thousands of people jamming the streets. I remember somebody putting me up on their shoulders so I could see better. But I really don't remember it that clearly."

"I thought you had lived here all your life," Paul said. "I can't believe you never came back to see it again."

"Don't forget, we lived down at the beach," Lisa reminded him, "until my mother married Dave."

"Why do you always get that funny look on your face and that tone in your voice when you mention his name?" Paul sounded annoyed.

"I didn't know that I did," she muttered.

"When are you going to grow up, Lisa? Your mother is married to Dave. She's been married to him for six months now. She's going to have his baby in a few months. Don't you think it's time you accepted the situation?"

Lisa couldn't believe what she was hearing. She had always known how Paul felt about her attitude toward Dave. But in the past, he had always tried to be sympathetic to her point of view too. Now he sounded just plain annoyed with her. She could sense he was losing his patience.

"I have tried to explain my point of view to you," she said stiffly. "You just don't seem to want to listen—"

"How can I help but listen," Paul interrupted. "It's all I ever hear from you. It's the only thing you ever talk about."

"That isn't true." She was getting more upset by the minute.

"Okay, let's go over it one more time," Paul said. "Maybe I've missed something along the way. You explain it to me." He sat back and folded his arms across his chest. "You tell me how you feel about it and I promise I won't say anything until you're finished."

"All right." Lisa paused for a moment to gather her thoughts. "It isn't that I have anything against Dave personally," she began.

Paul snickered, but he didn't say anything.

"In some ways, I guess he's really an okay guy. But he can't take the place of my real father."

Paul unfolded his arms and leaned forward, grabbing her hands. "But your own father never had a place in your life, Lisa. Why can't you understand that?"

Lisa snatched her hands back. "You promised you wouldn't interrupt me."

Paul shook his head slightly, but he settled back again in his chair without saying another word.

"Maybe that's the point," Lisa went on. "Maybe it's because my father never had a chance to be a part of our lives . . . maybe that's why I feel it's so unfair for Dave to just walk in and take over."

She could see that Paul was bursting with what he wanted to say, but he firmly bit his lip and let her go on.

"I guess I . . . I'm afraid . . . that if Dave takes over, we'll just forget my father. It will be as if he never existed."

"That's crazy," Paul burst out, unable to contain himself any longer. "The other day when I gave Peanuts to Holly for Christmas, and I told you to listen to what she was saying, what I meant was . . . just because Peanuts lives with us now doesn't mean that Holly's going to forget Scruffy. Did I forget my parents and Holly when I met you?"

"That's not exactly the same thing," Lisa said coldly.

"Of course it's the same thing," Paul argued. "I love my parents and I love Holly. Just because I love you doesn't mean I'm going to forget them."

A tingle of warmth coursed through Lisa at his words. She could see that Paul didn't even realize that he had said he loved her—he was so intent on trying to convert her to his point of view. But in seconds the glow had worn off as he went on.

"Love is expandable, Lisa. The more you love, the more you can love. Because you and your mother lived alone for so many years, I guess you never learned that. But she knows it. I know she must have loved your father. She certainly loves you. And now there's Dave and the new baby. It's just your own stubborn self that won't let you see that her loving them doesn't take anything away from you."

Lisa's head whirled with his words. She sat staring down at her hands folded on the table in front of her.

"Lisa." Paul's voice was gentle. "Can't you understand what I'm trying to tell you?"

She wanted to look up and tell him that she knew he was right. But it was so hard—hard to give up her unreasonable attitude toward Dave, hard to stop clinging to the picture of her father, hard to give up her childish image of her mother.

And then it was too late. Paul stood up slowly. "I feel

sorry for you, Lisa. You're going to mess up your whole life without ever realizing what you've done. Come on''—he motioned with his head—"I'll drive you home.''

He turned and walked up to the cashier to pay the bill and Lisa followed slowly behind. She wanted so badly to say something to him, to wipe that terrible resigned look from his face. But she was too confused herself to be able to explain anything to him.

Silently, they got back into the car and he drove the few short miles to her house. He swung the car in the driveway and leaned across to open the door so she could get out.

"I . . . I guess you won't be around at all tomorrow," she ventured. "I mean, you'll probably still be busy on the float."

"Probably," he muttered.

She slipped out of the car and turned to thank him, but before she could get the words out of her mouth, he said, "Good-bye, Lisa," and reached over and slammed the door.

The small car roared off down the street and Lisa stood watching as it disappeared into the dimness of the evening. The terrible finality of his last words echoed through her head. It had almost sounded as if he never wanted to see her again.

But that was ridiculous, she told herself, marching determinedly down the driveway to the back door. Tomorrow night was New Year's Eve; surely he would come over just to say Happy New Year. And besides, he had promised to pick her up early New Year's morning and take her to Tournament headquarters so that she could help the girls get dressed. Paul was always very aware of his obligations. He wouldn't let her down. And maybe by

the time she saw him tomorrow night her own thinking
would have straightened out and she'd be able to explain
her point of view so that he could finally understand it.
Although, to tell the truth, she was beginning to wonder
whether she understood it herself.

CHAPTER TWELVE

"Well, I'm off now," Potsy said, slipping her arms into the old fur coat that always made Lisa think of a pile of dirty feathers. "I've left some lovely little sandwiches for you in the fridge and there's a fruitcake in the pantry." She slipped on a pair of woolen gloves. "A Happy New Year to you all. God Bless."

Lisa's mother got up from her seat on the sofa to give the housekeeper a big hug and wish her well, while Dave bestowed a hearty kiss on her cheek and added his good wishes.

Lisa waited until they stepped back before slipping her arms around her friend and giving her a warm squeeze and hug. She hadn't had a chance to confide her latest problems to Potsy today, what with all the preparations for the big New Year's Day open house that her mother and Dave were giving. But as soon as this last holiday celebration was over she meant to corner Potsy in her kitchen and reveal the confusion and jumble of emotions that threatened to overwhelm her, that tainted her friendship with

Paul, and prevented any possibility of a future relationship, however limited, with Dave.

"I guess you aren't going out tonight, Lisa." Her mother eyed her daughter's old blue jeans and worn T-shirt. "Don't you and Paul have plans with Holly and Floffy?"

"Holly and Floffy are going to a party," Lisa mumbled. "And Paul . . . Paul has to do the last minute work on the float."

"Oh, that's right," her mother said. "I'd almost forgotten. What time do you have to be there?"

"Five-thirty in the morning," Lisa said.

"Good heavens," her mother groaned. "You'd better set your alarm. I'm sure I'll be fast asleep at that time of night. I hope you told Paul not to ring the doorbell when he picks you up."

"Ummm, yes, ah, I'm sure I did." Her eyes darted around the room, not able to look squarely at her mother. How could Lisa tell her that she didn't know whether she'd ever see Paul again in her entire life—never mind his picking her up to go to the parade. She saw Dave watching her with the cool, enigmatic look he always adopted in her presence. And as usual, he didn't enter into the conversation.

Lisa picked up a book from the table and flopped back in the big easy chair, turning sideways and slinging her legs over the padded arm.

"How come you two aren't going out tonight? I thought there'd be a big studio party or something."

"There is," her mother said. "But Dave and I thought we'd stay here and have a nice quiet evening in front of the fire. After all," she sounded almost shy, "this is our first New Year's Eve together."

148

Lisa sat up and started to close the book. "I guess I'll go to my room so you two can be alone."

"Lisa, please, I didn't mean that," her mother said, the hurt look appearing once more in her eyes.

"I know that, Mom," Lisa said gently. "I didn't mean that the way it sounded. Gosh, if I were a newlywed, I'd probably want to spend my first New Year's Eve alone with my husband too."

Her mother smiled, relief evident in her face. "That's ridiculous. We'd love to have you spend the evening with us. Dave, why don't you light the fire now and we can play some Scrabble. Would you like that, Lisa?"

Lisa hesitated for a moment. Her first instinct had been to get up and leave the room as if her feelings were hurt or she didn't want to spend the time with them. But she suddenly realized how childish that would seem. And the truth of the matter was, she did want to spend the evening with them, and a game of Scrabble sounded like fun.

"Of course I'd like that," she answered her mother. "I'll get the set."

Once the board was set up, they got down to the game in earnest. Lisa had always been a top English student and spelling was never a problem for her, but she found in Dave a worthy opponent. Sandra dropped out of the competition, leaving the two of them to battle it out. And a battle it was. There were several good-natured disputes over proper spellings, soon solved by a quick glance in the dictionary. The long, lonely evening Lisa had dreaded never materialized as time flew by, unnoticed, while the competition raged. In the end, pure luck gave Lisa the edge. Her last pick of letters was a well-rounded selection of vowels and consonants, while poor Dave got stuck with the q, z, and x.

"I give up," he groaned. "There's nothing I can do with these little darlings." He shook his head in mock dismay.

"Good, I accept your surrender." Lisa grinned at him wickedly.

"Oh, great, thanks a lot." He made a face at her. "Don't get too cocky, I'll get you next time." He looked at his watch. "Besides, it's almost midnight, time to toast the New Year. Turn on the TV, Lisa, and I'll get the champagne."

"Champagne! Wow!" Lisa jumped up to turn on the set.

"Not for you, young lady," her mother protested, laughing. "You can see the New Year in with a glass of iced tea."

Lisa turned the set to one of the major networks and when Dave came in with the drinks, they settled back to watch the celebration on the screen.

When the hour struck, they toasted each other and the New Year. Dave gave her mother a long, tender kiss and Lisa turned away, not from embarrassment or anger, but because the thought flashed through her mind that it was wonderful for people in love to be together at a time like this. And her sense of loneliness and loss was suddenly like a dark cloud hanging over her.

Her mother slipped out of Dave's arms and turned to give Lisa a hug and kiss. "Happy New Year, darling. I hope this will be a happy one for you."

Lisa could sense her mother's unspoken words, the knowledge that the last year had been one of the worst in Lisa's life.

"Yes, I'll drink to that," Dave added, tipping his glass in her direction. But he made no move to embrace her and

Lisa felt just the slightest bit let down.

Tonight had been the most pleasant evening she had spent with Dave since the marriage. The normal thing would have been for him to at least lean over and kiss her on the cheek, but Lisa knew it was her own fault that he no longer felt free to do that. And she realized the thought made her uncomfortable.

"Lisa, honey, if you don't get to bed soon you aren't going to have any sleep at all tonight." Her mother frowned slightly.

"I think it's time we all called it a night," Dave said, setting his glass down on the table. "We want to get up early and watch the parade, and then we have that house full of people coming at five o'clock. You need your rest."

"You're right." Sandra sighed. "But it's been such a lovely evening, I hate to see it end."

"It's just the start of a wonderful year, " Dave murmured, putting his arm around her and leading her out to the hall. "You get settled in and I'll close up the house."

"I'll help you," Lisa said. "Good night, Mom."

She picked up the empty glasses and crumpled napkins and carried them into the kitchen. When she came back into the living room, Dave was damping down the fire.

"I'll finish up, Lisa." He straightened up and snapped off one of the table lamps. "Shall I leave the front porch light on for Paul?"

"Yes, please," Lisa said. "And I'll try not to wake you and Mom when I leave."

"Fine." He nodded curtly in her direction. "Good night. Have a good time tomorrow." He disappeared toward his room.

Lisa decided to take a quick shower and put out the clothes she planned to wear in the morning. She knew she wouldn't be thinking too clearly at five o'clock, so she wanted to get everything organized now. As soon as she had finished and snuggled down under the warm covers and flipped off the light, a great wave of fatigue rolled over her and she was asleep in seconds.

When the sharp shrill of the alarm jolted her back to consciousness, she couldn't believe that almost five hours had passed. "Good grief," she groaned, sitting on the edge of her bed, trying to rub her eyes open. "You have to be crazy to get up this early, even if it is for the Rose Parade."

By the time she had splashed her face with cold water and brushed her teeth she felt a little more human. It only took a few minutes to slip into her clothes and tiptoe quietly out to the front of the house. She decided she'd better eat something—she had no idea when she'd be able to have a proper meal. In the kitchen, she poured herself a glass of milk and took a banana from the fruit bowl. That would have to hold her for several hours, she was sure. She tugged on her heavy car coat and went to the front door to wait.

By five-thirty she began to wonder if Paul was coming. At five-forty she knew that he wasn't. Dejected, she started back toward her room. She would have to call around and see if someone on the local committee was still at home and could give her a ride.

She had just picked up the hall phone to carry it on its long cord into her room when Dave suddenly appeared in the hallway.

"Is something wrong, Lisa? I thought you'd be gone long before this."

"I, uh," she stammered. "Paul . . . I guess he got held up. I mean . . ."

"Don't worry about it. I'll take you."

Before Lisa could answer, he hurried back into his room and returned in minutes, dressed in jeans and a heavy jacket, the car keys jangling in his hand.

"Come on, let's go."

They were silent as they went out to the garage and got into the car. But as they drove down the quiet street, Dave turned to look at her.

"Is something wrong between you and Paul, Lisa? I'm not trying to pry, but I have noticed that we've seen very little of him lately."

Lisa hung her head. "We had a disagreement."

Dave gave a small laugh. "You mean you had a fight. That's all right, everybody fights sometime in their relationship."

Lisa shook her head in the darkness. "No, actually we didn't have a fight. But Paul . . . Paul gave up on me, I guess."

For a moment there was silence, then Dave's voice came gently through the night. "Do you want to tell me about it?"

She slumped back wearily against the seat of the car. "There isn't a lot to tell. He just doesn't like me anymore. He thinks I'm selfish and stubborn." Tears started to flow down her cheeks. "He told me it was time I grew up and . . . and . . ."

"Hey, take it easy." Dave reached out and grasped her hand, squeezing it gently. "We all say things we don't mean when we're angry. I'm sure you'll be able to straighten this out with Paul. I have a lot of faith in you. You know, you're really quite a girl."

Lisa stared at him through the darkness. "Do you honestly think that about me?"

"Of course I do. You know I never lie to you."

She sat up, her hands clenched into tight fists against her jeans. "But I thought you hated me. I mean, I wouldn't blame you if you did. I know some of the things I've said and done have been awfully mean and horrible."

They were approaching Orange Grove Avenue now, which was blocked off to traffic. Dave pulled over along the curb on one of the side streets and parked.

"I've always thought you were a pretty terrific girl, Lisa. When your mother and I were first married I tried to tell you, but you never wanted to listen to anything I said." There was a trace of bitterness in his voice. He turned away from her to stare out through the windshield. "When I married your mother, I thought we were going to be one big happy family. I didn't have any children with my first wife and I thought I was getting a beautiful young daughter along with the most wonderful wife a guy could have." He smiled wryly in the dawning light. "But, like most dreams, it didn't work out exactly the way I planned."

"I'm sorry," Lisa whispered. "I've hurt you and . . ."

"Hey, listen." Dave seemed to pull himself together. "Everyone can't like everyone else. I should have learned that, at my age."

"But I do like you," Lisa said earnestly. "I mean, it has nothing to do with you personally. You've been very good to me and I know you love my mother. It's just . . ." She shook her head, wondering if he would understand any more than Paul did. "You . . . you're not my father."

"But I don't want to be your father. That's what you've never understood, Lisa. I want to be your friend. I've never asked that you love me, only that you like me." He looked at her intently. "Do you hate the thought of the new baby because the baby is mine?"

"No." Lisa's voice was so soft it could hardly be heard in the confines of the car. "I didn't want Mom to have another baby because I was afraid it would take my place." She felt the pressure of tears behind her eyes. "That's what the argument with Paul was about. He tried to make me see that I was wrong. He told me that love stretches for ever and ever, that it has no limits—that just because Mom will love the new baby doesn't mean she'll stop loving me."

Dave reached out and turned her face gently toward him. "And you're afraid that isn't true?"

"I don't know," she whispered, the tears spilling over and trickling down her cheeks. And suddenly she was leaning against Dave's shoulder, sobbing openly, his arms tight around her.

"Lisa, Lisa," he whispered above her ear. "You poor kid." He moved her slightly away from him. "Did you really think anything could change your mother's love for you?"

"I've been acting like a real crazy, haven't I?" she whispered. "I don't know what was wrong with me."

"I do." He lifted her chin, forcing her to look at him. "You were scared and worried and your whole life was being turned upside down. In a way, your mother and I were partly to blame. We love each other very much, Lisa, and I guess that blinded us somewhat to what was going on with you. I'm sorry that we let it happen."

Lisa dug in her purse for a tissue and wiped her wet cheeks. "Well," she said, a determined tone in her voice,

"I want you to know that that's all over now." She made a face. "It took a lot of talking from Potsy and Holly . . . and Paul." Her voice dropped when she mentioned the last name. "But they were right and I was wrong." She looked over at Dave. "I hope someday you can forgive me."

Dave squeezed her hand. "I hope someday you can accept me."

Lisa opened the car door and slid out. Just as she went to close the door, she leaned over and said, "I really do like you, Dave. And I think I probably have accepted you already. I just haven't had a chance to tell myself about it." She grinned at him, then waved and walked away, a buoyancy in her step that had been missing for a long time.

On Orange Grove Avenue the floats were already lined up in a long row. Lisa made her way into the Tournament of Roses building where the girls were donning their costumes. Once again the Japanese women were there to help, and as each girl's outfit was completed, Lisa took over, applying their makeup and helping to arrange their hair. At seven o'clock the girls went down to the street where they had to be lifted onto the float by a small forklift.

Lisa looked around at the display of magnificent flower-covered floats. Some of them were getting last-minute touches and repairs where flowers and greenery had been disturbed in the move to the parade site.

It was freezing cold in the early morning air. The girls on Lisa's float were wearing thermal underwear under their Japanese costumes, but some of the other floats had their princesses in skimpy evening gowns or sheer costumes. Lisa felt sorry for them, for once they had been lifted up into position on their floats, they had to remove the warm coats they had been wrapped in. Of course, once the sun came out they would be more comfortable, but at the moment Lisa could see that many of them were shivering and covered with goose bumps.

The bleachers lining Orange Grove Avenue and Colorado Boulevard were beginning to fill up, as spectators jockeyed for the best position to see the parade. In the TV booths on the corner, announcers and technicians had begun to assemble.

Pink and blue guidelines had been painted on the streets along the route for the floats to follow. The drivers were buried deep under the massive platforms and Lisa didn't envy them their jobs.

Before long the marching bands arrived and began to assemble in their proper places. The many equestrians and their horses, in colorful costumes and ribbons, took their places in line. Lisa searched the area for a glimpse of Paul, but he was nowhere in sight.

And then it was time. The Grand Marshal arrived in an open car with his family, and everything was ready for the annual Tournament of Roses Parade to begin.

The sun was shining and it was a beautiful, clear morning. Lisa hurried around the corner onto the boulevard, looking for an advantageous spot from which to watch the whole event. It was a breathtaking array, and even though their town float didn't win a prize, Lisa still watched proudly as it went by. She waved at the Japanese princesses high above her, and as they waved back, one of them called out, "Hi, Lisa."

Much later, when the last float and horse and rider had moved on down the boulevard, the crowd spilled out of the bleachers and milled around the streets. A row of motorcycle officers blocked off the end of the parade, keeping spectators from tagging along behind.

Lisa had just started back toward Tournament headquarters to see if she could hitch a ride home when she heard someone hail her from across the street. Peering over the mass of bodies that swarmed around her, she saw Holly on the opposite curb waving frantically. Lisa started to wave back when she suddenly spotted Paul standing just to Holly's left. And next to him was Kayla Morse.

The sight of Paul with the other girl was devastating. Lisa turned and ran down the block, pretending she hadn't heard Holly call her name. One of the other boys who had worked on the float was at headquarters and gave her a ride home.

When he let her out in front of her house, instead of going inside, she dashed across the lawn to the giant hedge, quickly burrowing her way into her secret hiding place.

The morning air was warmer now, but Lisa clutched her car coat closely around her as shivers ran through her body. A scratching noise outside the small hideout attracted her attention and she peered out to find Scruffy, pink tongue panting and fluffy white tail wagging. Right beside him stood Peanuts, in exactly the same position as the bigger dog, looking up at Scruffy with admiration, as if to say "am I doing this right?"

Lisa burst out laughing and then dissolved into tears as she tugged the two dogs onto her lap. She sat, hugging and rocking them, as she gave in completely to overwhelming feelings of remorse and loss.

CHAPTER THIRTEEN

Hunger finally drove Lisa into the house. The milk and banana she had downed at five o'clock were long gone and her stomach felt like a gaping cavern.

Her mother and Potsy were in the kitchen, busy with preparations for the party that afternoon.

"Hi, honey." Her mother greeted her with a big smile. "Good heavens," she exclaimed as she took a good look at Lisa. "You look terrible! Getting up in the middle of the night must not agree with you."

"I'm fine," Lisa muttered, lowering her head. She reached for a cheese-covered cracker. "I just need something to eat."

"Go shower and change your clothes, love," Potsy said. "I'll fix something for you while you're gone."

"I can do it." Lisa yanked open the refrigerator, reaching out just in time to grab a melon as it started to roll off the shelf.

"Lisa, please." Her mother sounded exasperated. "Mrs. Potter and I have a great deal of work to do this morning. You're just getting in our way."

Once again the treacherous tears welled. "I'm always in someone's way," Lisa cried. "No one wants me around. No one cares what happens to me." She knew she was giving in to hysteria but she couldn't help it. This had been one of the worst days of her life and it wasn't even half over yet. She spun around to run out of the room and crashed into the solidness of a man's body.

"It's okay, Lisa," Dave said softly, steadying her on her feet.

Lisa heard the inarticulate sound her mother made behind her, then Dave's voice, warm and reassuring.

"I'll take care of this, Sandra. It's all right. I understand the problem."

Lisa shot a quick glance over her shoulder and saw the distressed looks on the faces of her mother and Potsy. Dave's arm was around her shoulders and her mother reached out as if to caution him, but Lisa slumped against him, her fury suddenly gone.

"It's okay, Mom," she said wearily. "Dave knows all about it."

"About what?" her mother asked in confusion.

"I'll explain later." Dave turned to lead Lisa out of the room. "Right now I think Lisa needs to rest for a while."

He walked her to the door of her room.

"Will you be all right now?" He lifted her chin with his hand and she saw the look of kindly concern on his face.

Lisa nodded, a feeling of exhaustion descending over her. "I'm going to take a shower and lie down. I'll be okay, Dave. Don't worry about me."

His smile was comforting. "I'm not worried, Lisa. I told you before, I think you're quite a girl."

She squeezed his fingers, then abruptly went into her room and shut the door.

A warm shower and clean clothes made her feel a great deal better, and seemed to alleviate the terrible fatigue that had threatened to overcome her.

I have to be sensible about this, she thought as she pulled on a pair of warm knee socks and slipped into a pair of ankle boots. Paul is finished with me. I have to accept that. School starts again tomorrow and there's no way I can face everybody if they can see how I feel about it.

She walked over to her makeup table in front of the window to fix her face. She ran her hand gently over the wood, then snatched her fingers back, knowing that treacherous tears were not far away. But she refused to indulge herself in any more outbursts. So Paul had built the table for her . . . so what. She had to stop thinking about him every time she looked at it.

As she lifted the lid of the makeup kit and sat down to begin, a happier thought came to her. The day might have been a disaster as far as she and Paul were concerned, but there was no question that she and Dave had established a new relationship, and she had the feeling that it was on a firm basis. She might not have a new father, but she realized now that she did have a new friend.

Just as she finished applying her blusher, a loud rapping on her bedroom door brought her quickly to her feet.

"Lisa, can I come in?" It was Holly's voice calling to her from the hall.

Lisa snatched open the door. "Hi. Sit down. I was just going to put on some lipstick."

Holly draped herself across the end of the bed and watched as Lisa went on with what she had been doing. "I saw you up on the avenue this morning,'' Holly prattled. "I yelled and waved but I guess you didn't see me."

Lisa swallowed. "There were so many people," she murmured, not wanting to tell Holly a direct lie.

Holly sprawled on her back and clasped her hands behind her head. "Wasn't it gorgeous?" she exclaimed. "I think it was one of the best parades ever."

"And I thought our float was terrific," Lisa said, snapping the makeup box closed. "I don't understand why we didn't win a prize."

"Oh, well," Holly sighed. "They can't give a prize to everybody." She sat up and straightened her blouse. "Floffy's waiting in the den. We're going to go look at the floats. How about coming with us?"

Lisa looked at her warily. She wanted to ask if Paul was going along too. And if he was, was Kayla Morse part of the party? Lisa knew she couldn't stand that.

No, it was too much of a risk to take. From now on she had to forget about Paul and stay as far away from him as possible.

"I can't, Holly," she said. "My parents are having open house this afternoon and I have to be around to help."

Holly looked at her with a strange expression.

"What's the matter?" Lisa asked. "Don't you believe me? Your parents are invited, so they must know . . ."

"Sure," Holly said absently. "That isn't what puzzles me."

"Well, what then?" Lisa demanded, sure that Holly was going to say something about Paul.

"You said, 'my parents.' " Holly shook her head. "I've never heard you refer to Dave and your mother that way."

Lisa gave a surprised laugh. The words had slipped out without her even realizing it. "Well," she mumbled, "it gets kind of awkward trying to explain who Dave is. I mean . . . it's just easier this way . . ."

"Sure." Holly grinned at her happily. "I understand. Well"—she jumped up off the bed—"if you don't want to come, Floffy and I are going to go ahead. I'm sure the place will be mobbed so I want to get started."

Once the parade was over, all the floats were put on display in one central place, so that people could come and admire them for a few days before they were finally dismantled. Lisa would have liked to have seen them again, but not if it meant running into Paul and Kayla.

When Holly and Floffy had left, Lisa went into the kitchen to eat the snack Potsy had fixed for her.

"Save some room," her mother cautioned. "I'm sure you'll want to taste all the goodies we have ready for later."

"What time is everyone coming?" Lisa asked.

"Not until after the game," her mother said, knowing that most of their friends would want to be at home that afternoon to watch the Rose Bowl on television. "But I'm sure as soon as it ends, they'll all be over."

Lisa wandered into the den and found Dave settled in front of the TV set watching one of the eastern bowl games. When it was finally time for the Rose Bowl, at two o'clock, Lisa made a big batch of hot buttered popcorn, and she and Dave happily consumed the whole thing while watching the Pacific Coast team soundly beat their East Coast opponents.

By five o'clock they had changed their clothes and everything was ready when the first guests strolled in. It didn't take long for the house to fill up with a noisy, chattering crowd, and Lisa spent the next hour helping Potsy pass trays of hot hors d'oeuvres and spicy dips.

The doorbell rang at six-thirty and Lisa hurried to open it, wondering which of her mother's guests could be arriving so late. When she opened the door, she stared in astonishment at Paul, standing silently in front of her with a strange look on his face.

"H-hello," she stammered, all her well-controlled emotions scattering to the winds.

The muscles in his throat moved as he swallowed hard. "I'm going up to see the floats. I thought you might like to come with me."

"Again?" she asked.

Paul looked surprised. "What do you mean, again?"

"Didn't you go this afternoon with Holly and Floffy?" And Kayla Morse, she added silently.

"I've been in my room sleeping all afternoon." He reached out a tentative hand. "I've been awfully tired this week, Lisa. I guess that's why I said some things I shouldn't have." His fingers caressed her arm. "Hey, you're cold." He stepped into the house and shut the door behind him. "I think we need to talk, Lisa." He glanced toward the living room where the noise level and conversation were growing in volume. "Why don't you get your coat and ride up there with me?"

Lisa hesitated for a moment. "Are we going alone?"

"Of course. You just said Holly and Floffy have already been."

Lisa hung her head. "I didn't mean them, I meant—"

"Yeah." Paul let out a sigh. "I thought you saw me this morning with Kayla. You did, didn't you?"

Lisa nodded numbly.

"I told you a long time ago she doesn't mean anything

164

to me," Paul said earnestly. "I was watching the parade with Holly. Kayla just happened to come along and stand with us."

Lisa listened silently to his explanation.

"Why didn't you cross the street when Holly called to you?" he went on.

"I think you've forgotten something, Paul," Lisa said quietly. "You made it very clear when you brought me home the other night that you didn't want to see me anymore."

Paul looked astounded. "When did I say that?"

"You said . . . you said good-bye."

Paul looked at her for a long moment, then a rueful smile appeared on his lips. "And I made it sound final, didn't I?" he admitted. "I'm sorry, Lisa, but I was really upset with your attitude about things around here."

"You don't have to be anymore." She looked at him eagerly. "When you didn't come to pick me up this morning, Dave gave me a ride and . . . and we had a long talk about a lot of things. I really think we understand each other now. It's going to be a lot better from now on. Honest, Paul."

He reached out and grasped her shoulders. "I'm glad, Lisa. Glad for you. You know, you were making everybody around here miserable. But I think you were making yourself the most miserable of all." He gave her a small shake. "Come on, grab your coat and let's go."

Lisa ran to tell her mother where she was going, then followed Paul out to the waiting car. She still wasn't exactly sure how things stood between them. Paul had seemed pleased at her news about Dave, and he had tried to apologize for being impatient with her the last few days. But she still sensed a barrier between them and she didn't know how to get over or around it.

When they arrived at the site where the floats were on display, they strolled around, looking closely at all the intricate details, admiring the beauty of the flower-covered frames.

"I always feel sad when things like this are over," Lisa sighed. "All the work and energy that went into it and now it's over and soon it'll all be forgotten."

"Not forgotten," Paul said quietly. "It will always be a beautiful memory." He glanced at her sideways. "But I guess the memory hasn't been all that terrific for you, has it?"

Lisa shrugged. "You know that old saying, 'you learn from every experience.' " She thought back over the past weeks. "I've learned a lot since this holiday season began, even if it wasn't all good."

She *had* learned a lot. She had learned that even though someone may love you, their patience is not inexhaustible. She had learned that someone who loves you can hurt you more than anyone else in the world. She realized now how much she had hurt her mother over the past few months and she truly regretted much of what had happened. She had learned from Holly that love is indeed an infinite emotion stretching to include anyone and everyone you want it to.

But most of all she had learned that losing the one you love hurts more than anything else in the world.

Earlier in the morning she had been sure she'd lost Paul forever. But now . . . now she wasn't so sure. His bringing her here this evening—was it simply a neighborly gesture on his part, a slight atonement for the fact that he no longer considered her special? Or was it something else, something she hardly dared think about?

As they started to leave, Lisa turned back for one last look at the beautiful array on display. Paul reached out and grasped her wrist with tight fingers.

"Stand here for a minute," he said, "I forgot something." He dashed back to one of the floats, yanking a piece of greenery down, then ran back and held it over her head.

Lisa reached up to grab it. "What's this, a memento of the parade?"

Paul grinned down at her. "No, silly. Don't you know what that is?"

Lisa shook her head.

"It's mistletoe, you dope." Then he reached out and swooped her into his arms, giving her a hearty kiss. "I'm sorry about this morning," he whispered. "I know it was wrong of me not to pick you up."

Lisa hung her head, trying not to reveal how hurt she had been.

"I'll never do anything like that again," he promised. "From now on, we talk everything out . . . together." His arms tightened around her. "Happy New Year, Lisa. And it will be, I promise you."

Lisa flung her arms around his neck and hugged him tight. It was going to be a wonderful year. She could feel it in her bones. It might even turn out to be the best year of her life.

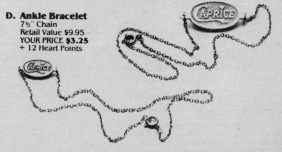

Now that you're reading the best in teen romance, why not make that *Caprice* feeling part of your own special look? Four great gifts to accent that "unique something" in you are all yours when you collect the proof-of-purchase from the back of any current *Caprice* romance!

Each proof-of-purchase is worth 3 Heart Points toward these items available <u>only</u> from *Caprice*. And what better way to make them yours than by reading the romances every teen is talking about! Start collecting today!

Proof-of-purchase is worth 3 Heart Points toward one of four exciting premiums bearing the distinctive *Caprice* logo

CAPRICE PREMIUMS
Berkley Publishing Group, Inc./Dept. LB
200 Madison Avenue, New York, NY 10016

PROOF OF
PURCHASE
—3—
HEART POINTS
♥ ♥ ♥
DETAILS INSIDE

MAGICQUEST™

A new fantasy series featuring
the best in Young Adult Fantasy—
classic titles of magic and
adventure by the top authors in
the fantasy field, in paperback
for the very first time!

THE THROME OF THE ERRIL OF SHERILL
by World Fantasy Award Winner
Patricia A. McKillip   _____ 80839-5/$2.25

THE PERILOUS GARD
A Newbery Honor Winner by
Elizabeth Marie Pope   _____ 65956-X/$2.25

THE SEVENTH SWAN
by the acclaimed British fantasist
Nicholas Stuart Gray   _____ 75955-6/$2.25

THE ASH STAFF
first of the Ash Staff series by
Paul R. Fisher   _____ 03115-3/$2.25

Available at your local bookstore or return this form to:

TEMPO
Book Mailing Service
P.O. Box 690, Rockville Centre, NY 11571

Please send me the titles checked above. I enclose _____. Include 75¢ for postage
and handling if one book is ordered; 25¢ per book for two or more not to exceed
$1.75. California, Illinois, New York and Tennessee residents please add sales tax.

NAME_____

ADDRESS_____

CITY_____ STATE/ZIP_____

(allow six weeks for delivery)   **T12**